H. C. Clark, Confederate States of America Constitution

The Confederate States Almanac

and repository of useful knowledge. For the year 1864 - being bissextile or leap year - the fourth of Southern independence - and, until July 4th, the eighty-eighth of the independence of the United States - Vol. 3

H. C. Clark, Confederate States of America Constitution

The Confederate States Almanac
*and repository of useful knowledge. For the year 1864 - being bissextile or leap year
- the fourth of Southern independence - and, until July 4th, the eighty-eighth of the
independence of the United States - Vol. 3*

ISBN/EAN: 9783337885403

Printed in Europe, USA, Canada, Australia, Japan

Cover: Foto ©Andreas Hilbeck / pixelio.de

More available books at **www.hansebooks.com**

VOL. THIRD.] [FIRST SERIES.

CONFEDERATE STATES

ALMANAC,

AND

REPOSITORY OF USEFUL KNOWLEDGE,

FOR THE YEAR

1864.

H. C. CLARKE,

PUBLISHER,

MOBILE, ALA............AUGUSTA, GA.

CONTENTS.

VOL. THIRD.]   [FIRST SERIES.

THE

CONFEDERATE STATES

ALMANAC,

AND

REPOSITORY OF USEFUL KNOWLEDGE.

FOR THE YEAR

1864:

Being FIRST XTILE or LEAP YEAR; the FOURTH of CONFEDERATE INDE-
PENDENCE, and, until July 4th, the EIGHTY-EIGHTH of the
INDEPENDENCE OF THE UNITED STATES.

Astronomical Calculations for the Latitude and Meridian of Augusta, Ga., and
Richmond, Va.,

BY T. P. ASHMORE, AMERICUS, GA.

COMPILED BY H. C. CLARKE,

MOBILE, ALA.

PREFACE.

The Third Volume of the Confederate States Almanac is now offered to the people of the South. The publisher is perfecting arrangements that will insure the permanent issue of the work every year. The leading object of the publication will be to make it the repository of the largest possible amount of useful information, embracing every variety of knowledge—annual statistics from all the States in the Confederacy, showing the progress in Population, Manufactures, Commerce, Wealth and all the elements of prosperity. The contents of this volume is not altogether perfect, or full, in some details of statistics.

Owing to the state of affairs in the country, the compiler found it impossible to obtain full Reports from all the States. Of the information contained in this volume, great pains has been taken to make them as accurate as possible from the resource at hand. The Reports of the Departments of the Confederate Government have been taken from the latest official documents, and will be found interesting.

Much valuable information has been compiled from the United States census of 1860, which will be found exceedingly interesting at the present time.

The Diary of the War and Incidents of the Revolution has been prepared with great care. The dates of the Battles will be found accurate; the number of killed and wounded in Battles, has been gathered from official Reports, as far as published. Although in most cases they have been estimated from statements of both sides, they will be found in the main to be nearly correct.

The Astronomical calculations, &c., have been prepared by Thomas P. Ashmore, of Georgia. The calculations will be found full and accurate. In a work like this, designed to embrace so much variety of matter, there is no doubt some errors. The compiler would be under obligations to the patrons of the work for any valuable hints, communications or corrections of errors, or improvements in the Almanac. Address the publisher.

Mobile, Ala., 1862.

SIGNS OF THE ZODIAC AND INFLUENCE OF THE MOON

THE Moon is supposed by some to have a special influence upon different parts of the bodies of men and animals, as it passes through the signs of the Zodiac. The following cut is inserted for the sake of those who believe in this imaginary influence, and is intended to represent the part of the body affected by the Moon when it is in any particular sign of the Zodiac. By finding the Moon's place in the proper column of the calendar pages, and comparing it with this cut, the particular part which is supposed to be affected, will be at once seen. Thus, when the Moon is in Aries (♈), it is supposed to influence the head and face; when in Capricornus (♑) the knees, etc.

♈ Governs the FACE and HEAD.

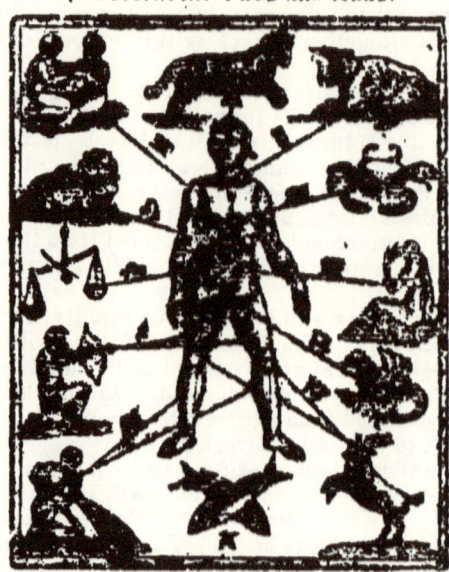

♊ ARMS.
♌ HEART.
♎ Reins.
♐ THIGHS.
♒ LEGS.

♉ NECK.
♋ BREAST
♍ BOWELS
♏ SECRETS
♑ KNEES.

♓ FEET.

NAMES AND CHARACTERS OF THE SIGNS OF THE ZODIAC.

♈ Aries, the Ram. ♉ Taurus, the Bull. ♊ Gemini, the Twins. ♋ Cancer, the Crab. ♌ Leo, the Lion. ♍ Virgo, the Virgin. ♎ Libra, the Balance. ♏ Scorpio, the Scorpion. ♐ Sagittarius, the Archer. ♑ Capricornus, the Goat. ♒ Aquarius, the Waterman. ♓ Pisces, the Fishes.

CHRONOLOGICAL CYCLES.

Dominical Letters,	C. & B.	Solar Cycle,	25
Golden Number,	3	Roman Indiction,	7
Epact, (Moon's age,) Jan. 1st	22	Julian Period	6577

MOVEABLE FEASTS OF THE CHURCH

Septuagesima Sunday	Jan. 24	Rogation Sunday,	May 1
Quin. or Shrove Sunday,	Feb. 7	Ascension Day,	May 5
Ash-Wednesday,	Feb. 10	Whit-Sunday,	May 15
Palm Sunday,	Mar. 20	Trinity Sunday,	May 8
Easter Sunday.	Mar. 27	Advent Sunday,	Nov 27

ECLIPSES FOR THE YEAR 1864.

During this year there will be only two Eclipses, and both of the Sun.

"The Moon her course doth so wisely steer,
That she runs in sunshine all this year."

The first will be of the Sun on the 5th of May, at 6h. 46m. P. M., invisible at Augusta, Ga. This Eclipse will be visible to all parts of North America. west of the Meridian of Houston in Texas. It will commence at Houston, Texas, about the time of sunset at that place. It will be annular and central in some places. and total in others. The diameter of the M[oon] viewed from the center of the Earth, will be just the size of that of the Sun; therefo[re] the central Eclipse at the times of sunrise and sunset will be annular; and the central Eclipse at noon will be total, but only for a few seconds.

The sun will rise centrally eclipsed in Lat. 3 deg. 44 m. North, and in Lon. 110 deg. 17 m. east of London. He will set centrally eclipsed in Lat. 25 deg. 14 m North, and in Lon. 113 deg. 18 m, west of London. The total Eclipse at noon, will be in Lat. 32 deg, 5 m. North, and in Lon. 173 deg. 30 m. East of London.

The second will be of the Sun on the 30th of October, at 9h. 58 m. A. M., invisible at Augusta, Ga.

This Eclipse will not be visible in any of the Confederate States except Texas, and the greatest Eclipse that will then be visible in that State, will be at the mouth of the Rio Grande; it will at that point amount to 1.7 digits only, on the Sun's south limb. The Moon's Penumbra will not quite reach New Orleans: it will pass about the mouth of the Mississippi river, and near Cape Sable in Florida. At the last two places, an apparent contact of limbs will take place only. This Eclipse will be annular. The Sun will rise centrally eclipsed in Lat 2 deg. 46m. North, and in Long. 117 deg. 16 m. west of London. He will set centrally eclipsed in Lat 23 deg. 9m S. and in Long. 11 deg. 21 m, east of London. The central Eclipse at noon, will be in Lat. 24 deg. 58m. S and in Lon. 57 deg. 35m west of London. The latter place is near the city of Assumption, in South America.

ASPECTS OF THE PLANETS.

The Planet Mercury will be visible on the morning of the 27th of February, about one hour before sunrise, in the Eastern sky. And again he will be visible in the Western sky, on the 17th of August, about one hour after sunset.

Venus will be Morning Star till the 18th of July, then Evening Star till the expiration of the year. Mars will pass through opposition with the Sun on the 24th of November. He will then be nearly as bright as Venus, and can be easily distinguished by his red color. Jupiter will be in opposition with the Sun on the 13th of May. Saturn will be in opposition with the Sun on the 4th of April.

At each conjunction of the Moon with the Planet Jupiter, during this year, she will pass, apparently very near him. She will pass to the south of him till the month of October, then to the North of him, till the end of the year. There will be several occultations of this Planet by the Moon during this year, but none of them will be visible in this country.

At each conjunction of the Moon with the Planet Saturn during this year, she will pass to the South of him.

NOTE.—The calculations of this Almanac are made to Solar or Apparent Time, to which add the Equation of Time given at the top of each calendar page, when the Sun is slow, and subtract it when he is fast for the Mean or Clock Time.

EXPLANATION OF THE SIGNS USED IN THIS ALMANAC.

● New Moon, and Moon generaly, ☾ First Quarter, ☉ Full Moon, ☽ Last Quarter. ☊ Moon's ascending node, or dragon's head. ☋ Moon's descending node, or dragon's tail. IN APOGEE—Moon farthest from the Earth. IN PERIGEE—Moon nearest the earth. ● Highest—Moon farthest North. ● Lowest—Moon farthest South. ♄ Saturn. ♀ Venus ☌ near together. ♃ Jupiter. ☿ Mercury □ 90 deg. apart. ☍ Opposition or 180 degrees apart. ♂ Mars. 7* Stars. ☼ Sun. ♅ Herschel.

COMETS.

Table of the most remarkable Cometary Bodies seen since the Christian Era:

Lengths of Tails Comet of B. C.	in deg	and miles	years	size of the following Comets.
" A. D.	371	694	114,000,000	
" " "	1450	69	70,000,000	Diam. in Miles.
" " "	1618	104	65,000,000	1778 830 Miles
" " "	1680	70	123,000,000	1805 869 "
" " "	1689	63	100,000,000	1799 4623 "
" " "	1744	30	35,000,000	1807 6360 "
" " "	1769	90	45,000,000	1811 4339 "
" " "	1811	23	132,000,000	1858 5000 probably.
" " "	1813	60	130,000,000	

TABLE OF SOME OF THE PRINCIPAL BODIES IN THE SOLAR SYSTEM.

NAMES.	Mean Diameter.	Mean Distance from the Sun.	Revolution r'd he Sun.	Revolution on Axis.	Velocity per m. in orbit.	Size—the Earth being 1.	Density the Earth b'ng 1	Light, Earth b'ng 1
	Miles.	Miles.	yrs. da.	d h. M.	Miles.			Ins.
The Sun..	883,246	....	25	9 59	....	1,412,921,101	0.252	rite.
Mercury..	3,224	36,814,000..	85	1 0 5	1,827	0,053	1.120	6 668
Venus....	7,657	68,757,000..	..224 ..	23 21	1,338	0,909	0,928	1.911
The Earth	7,912	95,113,000	1 ...	23 56	1,138	1,000	1.000	1.000
The Moon	2,190	95,103,000	1 ...27	7 43	38	0,020	0.816	1.000
Mars	4,190	144,908,000	1 321	1 0 37	921	0,125	0.948	0.431
Jupiter...	89,170	494,797,000	11 215	.. 9 56	496	1,456,000	0.238	0.037
Saturn....	79,042	907,168,000	29 167	10 29	368	771,000	0.138	0.010
Uranus...	35,112	1,824,290,000	84 6	1 15 33	259	89,000	0.242	0.000
Neptune..	41,500	2,854,000,000	164 223	.. ..	203	143,000	0.140	0.010

NOTE—There are more than fifty small Planets or Asteroids, between the orbits of Mars and Jupiter.

EQUINOXES AND SOLSTICES.

Vernal Equinox, ...(Spring begins) ....March 31st
Summer Solstice,..............(Summer begins) ....June 21st.
Autumnal Equinox, ...(Autumn begins) ....Sept. 23d.
Winter Solstice,.............(Winter begins). ....Dec. 21st.

ANSWERS TO THE PROBLEMS FOR 1863.

Problem 1st, 26-65 feet *Prob. 2d, 90 66 feet. Prob. 3d, 2 767. Prob. 4th, 700 lbs.* Prob. 5 h. 8 640 cubic inches. Prob. 6th, 9 ft Prob. 7th, 18 ft. Prob. 8th, 2*5 ft Prob 9th, 256 feet Prob. 10th, 12 649 ft Prob 11th, 176 ft. Prob. 12th 49 ft Prob. 13th, 68 seconds Prob. 14th, 118 ft Prob. 15th, 3750 lbs. Prob. 16th 6 224 ft. Prob 17th, 1656 86 miles. Prob, 18th, 4 ft.

* Problem 4th was a misprint. It should have been printed thus: 26.65.

MATHEMATICAL ACKNOWLEDGMENTS FOR 1863.

The problems for 1863 have been ably managed by the following named Mathematicians, whose solutions are here indicated:

Mr. J E Cartlidge, Newton, Miss.—Problems, 1, 2, 3, 4, 5, 6, 7, 8, 9, 10, 11, 12. 13, 14, 15, 16, 17, 18.

Mr Samuel F Saunders, Scarborough, Ga.—Problems, 1, 2 nearly, 3, 4, 5, 6, 7, 8, 9, 10, 11, 12, 13, 15, 16, 17, 18.

Mr B F. Sitton, Gainesville, Ga.—Problems, 1, 2 nearly, 3, 4, 5, 6, 7, 8, 9, 10 11, 12, 13, 15, 16, 17, 18.

Mr. George Maxey, Confederate Army, Richmond, Va.—Problems 1, 2, 3, 4, 5 nearly, 6, 7, 8, 9, 10, 11, 12, 13 15, 16, 17, 18.

Mr. Wm. O. Shields, Missionary Station, Ga.,—Problems, 2 nearly, 3, 7, 8, 11, 12, 13, 15, 16, 17, 18,

Mr. B. M. Sweet, Dawson, Ga.—Problems, 3, 5, 6, 7, 8, 9, 10, 11, 12, 13, 15, 17, 18, 16

Mr. Abram Evans, Confederate Army, Goldsboro', N. C.—Problems, 3, 6, 7, 10, 11, 12, 13, 15 nearly, 16, 17, 18.

Mr. John R. Cain, Americus, Ga.—Problems, 3, 5, 8, 11, 12, 13, 15, 16, 17, 18.

Several other persons have solved a few of the problems, but not enough to entitle their solutions to acknowledgment.

PROBLEMS FOR 1864.

The nine following Problems have been proposed by Mr. Samuel F. Saunders, Scarborough, Ga:

Prob. 1.—What is the length of a straight line that divides a circle 60 rods in diameter, into two parts whose areas are as 2 to 7 ?

Prob. 2.—Given the chord 4: and the arc 60, to find the versed sine.

Prob. 3.—In a square garden there is a spring, from which to three corners, there are 8, 9 and 7 rods; how far is it from the other corner?

Prob. 4.—From a spring in a square field to the corners, are 23, 33, 27 and 18 rods, what is the area?

Prob. 5.—If the diameter of the directing circle be 80, and the generating circle 10, what is the area of each epicycloid ?

Prob 6. —If a circle 4 feet in diameter, roll around another circle of the same diameter; what will be the area and curve generated by a point in the circumference?

Prob. 7.—The two lines that bisect the acute angles of a right-angled triangle, are A and B; what are the lengths of the sides of the triangle?

Prob. 8—In a right-angled triangle there are given the side of the inscribed square, and the radius of the inscribed circle, to find the sides.

Prob. 9.— The diameter of a conical tree is 4 feet, its height is 90 feet; if a squirrel run spirally 40 times around it in going up, how far will it travel ?

The four following Problems have been proposed by Mr. J. E. Cartlidge, Newton, Miss.

Prob. 10.—What is the difference between the major and minor proportional differences of 5 and 6, and the difference of their numerical value?

Prob. 11.—What is the difference between the area of a circle whose radius is 50, yards, and its greatest inscribed square?

Prob. 12.—I have an orchard of int 9 trees, which are set in 9 rows, with 3 in each row. Required a diagram representing the orchard.

Prob. 13.—A. B and C. purchase a grindstone 30 inches in diameter; A paid $2; B $3, and C $1. according to agreement. A grinds off his share first, then B, and C. last, how many inches in diameter must A and B each grind off, to leave C his proportional share, making no allowance for the eye of the stone?

The following Problem has been proposed by Mr. W. C. Shields. Missionary Station, Ga.

Prob 14.—In a circle containing just 500 acres, three other equal circles are inscribed as large as they possibly can be, touching, but not cutting each other ; what is the area of each small circle, and what distance apart are their centres, and what distance is between each of their center, and the center of the large circle, and how much land is left in the large circle, not included in the three small ones?

I propose the following Problems:

Prob. 15.—If the sun's true Longitude be L., and the Obliquity of the Ecliptic be E, what will be his Right Ascension and Declination?

Prob. 16.—When the sun's true Longitude is 60 deg. what is the Equation of Time ?

Prob. 17.—What is the difference between the sine of an arc of 1 sec. and the tangent of the same arc of 1 sec. radius being 1?

Prob. 18.—At what hour and minute will the sun rise on the 21st of June, in Lat. 50 degrees North?

Prob. 19.—When the moon's Lon. is twenty degrees, and her Lat. 3 degrees N. what is her right Ascension and Declination?

Prob. 20.—If the eccentricity of a Planet's orbit be 0.25604 ; what is the greatest equation of the center, and what is the Equation when the mean Anomaly equals 90 degrees?

Prob. 21.—If the periodical time of a Primary Planet be P, and the periodical time of its Satellite be p, and if the distance of the Planet from the sun be D, and the distance of the Satellite from the Planet be d; what will be the mass of the Primary Planet, the sun's mass being 1?

Prob. 22.—When the distance of a Comet moving in a parabolic orbit, is the same from the sun as that of the Earth, with what velocity will the Comet move, the velocity of the Earth being 68,000 miles per hour.

NOTE.—Any person solving ten of the above problems, and sending to me at Americus, Ga. by the 15th of May next, the correct answers to the same, shall have the same acknowledged in the Almanac for 1865. A few nice original Problems are desired for 1865. They must be of the higher order, and solvable only by the higher branches of Analysis. They must be thoroughly solved and explained, in order to meet with attention.   T. P. ASHMORE.

Showing the Rising and Setting of the Sun—Lat. 37 deg 32 m. N, Long: 77 deg 27 m. W

1st Month   JANUARY, 1864   31 days

MOON'S PH.	D.	H. M.		EQUATION OF TIME.
Last Quarter,	1	9 47 eve.		
New Moon,	9	2 3 mo.	Sun slow.	37 ...
First Quarter,	15	11 4 eve.		
Full Moon,	23	4 13 eve.		
Last Quarter,	31	1 30 eve.		

D. of M.	D. of W.	Various Phenomena.	Sun rises H. M.	Sun sets H. M.	Moon's Place	Moon rises & sets H. M.	Moon souths & van. h. M.
1	Frid	New Year's Day. *Cold*	7 4	4 56	♎	Morn.	5 0
2	Satur	Sun in Perigee *and*	7 3	4 57		0 5	3 45
3	S	♀ rises 4h 4m *windy*	7 3	4 57	♏	1 13	4 24
4	Mon	♃ rises 3h 32m	7 3	4 57		2 40	5 0
5	Tues	Moon ☌ ♃ & ♀ 6h 36m mo	7 2	4 54	♐	4 0	6 6
6	Wed	Epiphany *Cloudy and*	7 2	4 59		5 14	7 16
7	Thur	Moon lowest	7 2	4 58	♑	6 7	7 58
8	Fril	Skirm Silver Creek, '62	7 1	4 59		6 45	8 41
9	Satur	Col Lubbock died, 1862	7 1	4 59		sets	9 22
10	S	Battle Prestonburg, '62	7 0	5 0	♒	6 40	10 1
11	Mon	Moon in Perigee *rainy*	7 0	5 0		7 52	10 41
12	Tues	♀ rises 3h 59m	6 59	5 1	♓	9 0	11 18
13	Wed	Cherokee Mission es '17	6 59	5 1		10 12	morn
14	Thur	Aldebaran sou 8h 52m	6 58	5 2		11 20	0 16
15	Frid	*Fair and frosty morn*	6 58	5 2	♈	morn	0 46
16	Satur	Battle Ironton, 1862	6 57	5 3		0 30	1 32
17	S	Battle Cowpens, 1781	6 57	5 3	♉	1 31	2 24
18	Mon	Ex-president Tyler d '62	6 56	5 4		2 25	3 26
19	Tues	Battle Mill Springs '61	6 55	5 5		3 15	4 39
20	Wed	Sun enters ♒.	6 55	5 5	♊	4 5	5 55
21	Thur	Capella sou 9h 3m	6 54	5 6		4 50	7 10
22	Frid	Moon highest	6 54	5 6	♋	5 41	8 8
23	Satur	*Cloudy and cold*	6 53	5 7		rises	9 0
24	S	Septuagesima Sunday	6 52	5 8	♌	6 10	9 45
25	Mon	♀ ☌ Sun, Inferior.	6 51	5 9		7 15	10 26
26	Tues	Sirius sou 10h 10m	6 51	5 9	♍	8 20	11 2
27	Wed	*Perhaps snow or sleet*	6 50	5 10		9 18	11 38
28	Thur	Peter the Great died 1725	6 49	5 11	♎	10 12	eve 14
29	Frid	Prof. Bond died, 1859	6 49	5 12		11 2	0 47
30	Satur	Gt Eastern launched '59	6 48	5 12	♏	11 55	1 24
31	S	Sexagesima Sunday	6 47	5 13		Morn	2 2

2d Month FEBRUARY, 1864 29 days

MOON'S PHASES.	D.	H.	M.	
New Moon	7	0	43	eve.
First Quarter	14	1	4	eve.
Full Moon	22	11	22	mo.

Sun slow

EQUATION OF TIME.

D.	1	5	9	13	17	21	25	29
M.	13	14	14	14	14	13	13	12
S.	49	15	20	29	18	56	23	41

D. of M	D. of W	Various Phenomena.	Sun rises H. M.	Sun sets H. M.	Moon's Place	Moon ri. st. H. M.	High tide Savannah. H. M.
1	Mon.	Skirmish at Bloomey,	6 46	5 14	♐	0 44	2 46
2	Tue.	1862. *High winds*	6 45	5 15		1 47	3 47
3	Wed.	Fort Henry attac'd, '62.	6 44	5 16		2 51	5 0
4	Thu.	*from N. W. and cold.*	6 44	5 16	♑	3 52	6 21
5	Fri.	Earthq'ke at Sicily, 1780	6 43	5 17		4 48	7 30
6	Satu.	*Fair and frosty.*	6 42	5 18	♒	5 58	8 16
7	*S.*	Shrove Sunday.	6 41	5 19		sets.	9 2
8	Mon.	Roanoke Isl'd taken, '62	6 40	5 20		6 43	9 45
9	Tue.	Federals at Florence, '62	6 39	5 21	♓	7 45	10 25
10	Wed.	Ash Wed. *N. E. winds.*	6 38	5 22		8 50	11 5
11	Thu.	Rev. St. Domingo, 1807.	6 37	5 23	♈	9 58	11 45
12	Fri.	*with many dark clouds.*	6 30	5 24		11 0	morn.
13	Sat.	Bat. Fort Donelson, 62.	6 36	5 24		11 55	0 28
14	*S.*	St. Valentine's Day.	6 35	5 25	♉	morn.	1 13
15	Mon.	Sirius sou. 8h 42m.	6 34	5 26		0 31	1 50
16	Tue.	Fort Donelson sur. 1862	6 33	5 27	♊	1 15	2 57
17	Wed.	Provis. Con. ended, 1862	6 32	5 28		2 0	4 9
18	Thu.	☾ highest. *Cloudy*	6 31	5 29	♋	2 44	5 34
19	Fri.	Sun enters ♓	6 30	5 30		3 25	6 58
20	Sat.	*and damp weather.*	6 29	5 31	♌	4 35	8 1
21	*S.*	Moon in Apogee.	6 28	5 32		5 45	8 40
22	Mon.	Jeff. Davis, inaug. 1862	6 27	5 33	♍	rises.	9 32
23	Tue.	Bat. Buena Vista, 1849	6 26	5 34		7 1	10 9
24	Wed.	Nashville surren. 1862.	6 25	5 35	♎	7 45	10 43
25	Thu.	*Much cloudy weather*	6 24	5 36		8 31	11 14
26	Frid.	☿'s greatest elong. W.	6 23	5 37	♏	9 15	11 46
27	Satu.	☿ visible morn. *may now*	6 22	5 38		10 6	E 15
28	*S.*	♉ 8° 5′ east of ♀.	6 21	5 39		11 0	0 49
29	Mon.	☾ ☌ ♃ *be expected.*	6 21	5 39	♐	11 55	1 24

3d Month. MARCH, 1864 31 days

MOON'S PH.	D.	H.	M.	
Last Quarter	1	2	38	mo.
New Moon	7	10	58	eve.
First Quarter	15	4	26	mo.
Full Moon	23	4	54	mo.
Last Quarter	30	1	22	eve.

Sun slow.

EQUATION OF TIME.

D.	M.	S.
1	12	29
5	11	36
9	10	37
13	9	32
17	8	23
21	7	11
25	5	58
29	4	44

D. of M.	D. of W.	Various Phenomena.	Sun rises H.	M.	Sun sets H.	M.	Moon's Place.	Moon ri. & sets H.	M.	High tide Savan'ah H.	M.
1	Tues	♀ rises 4h. 36m.	6	20	5	40	♐	morn.		2	4
2	Wed	*Cloudy and damp.*	6	19	5	41	♑	1	0	2	53
3	Thur	Mar. Law in Richm.'62	6	18	5	42		2	21	4	8
4	Frid	Pollux sou. 8h 44m.	6	17	5	43	♒	3	30	5	29
5	Satur	*Many flying Clouds.*	6	16	5	44		4	42	6	47
6	*S.*	Moon in Perigee.	6	15	5	45		5	31	7	52
7	Mon	Bat. Pea Ridge, 1862	6	14	5	46	♓	sets.		8	37
8	Tues	Bat. near Norfolk, '62	6	13	5	47		6	25	9	22
9	Wed	Confed. army leave	6	12	5	48	♈	7	20	10	2
10	Thur	Manassas.	6	11	5	49		8	12	10	44
11	Frid	Surnames first used 1072	6	10	5	50		9	2	11	27
12	Satur	*Rainy and stormy.*	6	9	5	51	♉	9	56	Morn.	
13	*S.*	♅ discovered, 1781.	6	8	5	52		10	44	0	16
14	Mon	*Cold enough for ice.*	6	7	5	53	♊	11	35	0	54
15	Tues	Is. No. 10 attack'd, 1862	6	6	5	54		morn.		1	41
16	Wed	Regulus sou. 10h. 31m.	6	5	5	55		0	26	2	36
17	Thur	☾ highest. St. Patrick.	6	4	5	56	♋	1	24	3	49
18	Frid	Vega rises 10h. 26m.	6	3	5	57		2	15	5	16
19	Satur	*Stormy and unpleasant.*	6	2	5	58	♌	3	6	6	40
20	*S.*	☾ in Apogee, Palm Sun.	6	1	5	59		3	48	7	43
21	Mon	☉ enters ♈. Days and	6	0	6	0	♍	4	35	8	29
22	Tues	[nights equal.	5	59	6	1		5	23	9	10
23	Wed	Battle Kearnstown, '62.	5	58	6	2	♎	rises.		9	43
24	Thur	*Much rain may now be*	5	57	6	3		7	15	10	17
25	Frid	Good Friday.	5	56	6	4	♏	8	6	10	46
26	Satur	Lady's day.	5	55	6	5		9	3	11	17
27	*S.*	Easter Sunday.	5	54	6	6	♐	9	57	11	48
28	Mon	Easter Monday.	5	53	6	7		10	48	Ev.	18
29	Tues	☽ lowest. *expected.*	5	52	6	8	♑	11	42	0	50
30	Wed	Regulus sou. 9h. 26m.	5	51	6	9		morn		1	30
31	Thur	♄ rises 6h. 26m.	5	50	6	10		0	35	2	19

4th Month   APRIL, 1864   30 days

MOON'S PHASES.			
	D. H. M.		
New Moon	6 8 49 mo.		
First Quarter	13 8 27 eve.		
Full Moon	21 7 55 eve.		
Last Quarter	28 10 0 eve		

EQUATION OF TIME. — Sun slow.

D. of M	D. of W	Various Phenomena.	Sun rises H.M.	Sun sets H.M.	Moon's Place	Moon rises H. M.	High tide Savannah H. M.
1	Frid	All Fool's Day. *Fair*	5 49	6 11	≈	1 31	3 24
2	Satur	☾ in Perigee.	5 48	6 12		2 28	4 51
3	S	Low Sunday.	5 47	6 13	✶	3 21	6 11
4	Mon	♄ ☌ ☉. ♄ ri. at sunset.	5 46	6 14		4 20	7 18
5	Tues	*Cloudy and some rain.*	5 45	6 15		5 15	8 8
6	Wed	Battle Shiloh, 1862.	5 44	6 16	♈	sets.	8 53
7	Thur	Island No. 10 sur. 1862.	5 43	6 17		7 37	9 35
8	Frid	*Fine weather for*	5 42	6 18	♉	8 29	10 21
9	Satur	Ed. IV. died 1483.	5 41	6 19		9 22	11 4
10	S.	Bat. of Toulouse, 1814.	5 40	6 20	□	10 12	11 51
11	Mon	Fort Pulaski surren. '62	5 39	6 21		11 4	Morn.
12	Tues	Regulus sou. 8h. 35m.	5 38	6 22		11 57	0 34
13	Wed	☾ highest. *planting.*	5 37	6 23	♋	morn.	1 24
14	Thur	Embargo repealed 1814	5 36	6 24		0 42	2 21
15	Frid	☉ and clock agree.	5 35	6 25	♌	1 28	3 29
16	Satur	☾ in Apogee. *Cool*	5 34	6 26		2 15	4 54
17	S.	Virginia seceded, 1861.	5 33	6 27	♍	3 6	6 11
18	Mon	Spica sou 11h. 27m.	5 32	6 28		3 40	7 16
19	Tues	Bat. Lexington, 1775.	5 11	6 29	♎	4 25	8 4
20	Wed	Sun enters ♉. *days and*	5 30	6 30		5 0	8 42
21	Thur	*light frosts expected.*	5 29	6 31	♏	rises.	9 16
22	Frid	♉'s greatest elonga'n E.	5 28	6 32		7 35	9 48
23	Satu	St. George.	5 27	6 33	♐	8 33	10 19
24	S.	Brazil discovered, 1500	5 26	6 34		9 26	10 49
25	Mon	Ft. Jackson surren. '62.	5 25	6 35		10 15	11 20
26	Tues	*Fair and*	5 24	6 36	♑	11 2	11 42
27	Wed	Fed. troops at N. O. '62.	5 23	6 37		11 48	E. 27
28	Thur	Wolfe killed, 1759.	5 22	6 38	≈	morn.	1 8
29	Frdi	*pleasant*	5 21	6 39		0 40	1 57
30	Satur	Washington inaug. '89.	5 20	6 40	✶	1 25	2 58

5th Month — MAY, 1864 — 31 days

MOON'S PHASES.

	D.	H.	M.
New Moon	5	6	46 eve.
First Quarter	13	0	47 eve.
Full Moon	21	7	49 mo.
Last Quarter	28	5	19 mo.

Sun fast.

EQUATION OF TIME.

M. S. — 5 30, 46, 53, 51, 39, 19, 51

D of M	D of W	Various Phenomena.	Sun rise H.M.	Sun sets H.M.	Moon's	Moon ri. & st. H. M.	High tide Savannah H. M.
1	S.	Rogation Sunday.	5 20	6 40	♍	2 14	4 18
2	Mon	Spica sou, 10h 38m.	5 19	6 41		3 0	5 33
3	Tues	Tennessee seceded '61.	5 18	6 42	♈	3 52	6 43
4	Wed	*Fair and mild.*	5 17	6 43		4 44	7 37
5	Thur	☾ Eclipsed invisible.	5 16	6 44	♉	sets.	8 29
6	Frid	Bat. Williamsburg, '62	5 15	6 45		7 47	9 11
7	Satur	Bat. West Point, Va.'62	5 15	6 4?		8 30	9 59
8	S.	Trinity Sunday.	5 14	6 46	♊	9 15	10 47
9	Mon	♃ rises 7h 8m.	5 13	6 47		9 52	11 32
10	Tues	*Warm and dry*	5 12	6 48	♋	10 31	Morn.
11	Wed	Virginia blown up 1862	5 12	6 48		11 3	0 17
12	Thur	Moon in Apogee.	5 11	6 49	♌	11 36	1 5
13	Frid	*Cloudy and a fine grow-*	5 10	6 50		morn.	2 1
14	Satur	*ing season may now be*	5 9	6 51	♍	0 6	3 2
15	S.	Whit-Sunday. *expected.*	5 9	6 51		0 41	4 15
16	Mon	Whit-Monday.	5 8	6 52	♎	1 20	5 26
17	Tues	Rev in Venice, 1767.d	5 7	6 53		2 4	6 32
18	Wed	Arcturus sou 10h 21m	5 7	6 53		2 48	7 2
19	Thur	*Rain with wind and*	5 6	6 54	♏	3 21	8 6
20	Frid	Sun enters ♊. *thunder.*	5 5	6 55		4 35	8 46
21	Satur		5 5	6 55	♐	rises.	9 20
22	S.	☿ ☌ Sun, Inferior.	5 4	6 56		8 25	9 53
23	Mon	Irish rebellion com. '98.	5 4	6 56	♑	9 8	10 25
24	Tues	Bat. Front Royal, 1862.	5 3	6 57		9 50	10 59
25	Wed	Bat. Winchester, 1862.	5 3	6 57	♒	10 31	11 38
26	Thur	Bom. Vicksburg. 1862.	5 2	6 58		11 10	E. 9
27	Frid	Arcturus sou 0h 46m.	5 2	6 58		11 45	2 52
28	Satur	*Pleasant weather.*	5 1	6 59	♓	morn.	1 42
29	S.	Corinth ev. by Confed.	5 1	6 59		0 10	2 38
30	Mon	Alex. Pope died, 1744.	5 0	7 0		0 40	3 46
31	Tues	Bat. Seven Pines, 1862.	5 0	7 0	♈	1 15	4 59

6th Month JUNE. 1864 30 days.

MOON'S PHASES.					EQUATION OF TIME.
	D.	H.	M		
New Moon	4	5	56 mo.		
First Quarter	12	5	22 mo.		
Full Moon	19	5	15 eve.		
Last Quarter	26	9	1 eve.		

Sun fast.

D. of M	D. of W	Various Phenomena.	Sun rises H.M.	Sun sets H.M.	MOON'S PLACE	Moon ri &ts M.	Moon ri &ts N.	High tide Savannah M.
1	Wed	Bat. Seven Pines end. '62	4 59	7 1	♉	2	5	6 4
2	Thur	Arcturus sou 9h 27m.	4 59	7 1		2	50	7 6
3	Frid	Transit of ♀ in 1769.	4 59	7 2	♊	3 43	8	-1
4	Satur	*Rainy weather* and	4 58	7 2		sets.	8	51
5	S.	Moon highest *a fine*	4 58	7 2	♋	8 21	9	44
6	Mon	Bat. Memphis, 1862.	4 57	7 3		9 3	10	32
7	Tues	W B Mumford hung, '62	4 57	7 3	♌	9 38	11	16
8	Wed	Moon in Apogee.	4 57	7 3		10 11	Morn.	
9	Thur	Bat. Pt. Republic, 1862.	4 57	7 3		10 42	0 16	
10	Frid	Victory Bethel Ch. '61.	4 56	7 4	♍	11 20	0 59	
11	Satur	St. Barnabas *growing*	4 56	7 4		11 56	1 33	
12	S.	N. York incorp. 1665.	4 56	7 4	♎	Morn.	2 30	
13	Mon	*season may now*	4 56	7 4		0 44	3 22	
14	Tues	Arcturus sou. 8h. 37m.	4 56	7 4	♏	1 30	4 25	
15	Wed	Sun and clock agree.	4 56	7 4		2 6	5 37	
16	Thur	*take place.*	4 55	7 5	♐	2 34	6 36	
17	Frid	Bat. Bunker Hill, 1775.	4 55	7 5		3 21	7 31	
18	Satur	Bat. Waterloo, 1815.	4 55	7 5		4 10	8 14	
19	S.	Moon lowest. *Warm*	4 55	7 5	♑	rises.	8 54	
20	Mon	Q. Vict. crowned, '37.	4 55	7 5		7 28	9 29	
21	Tues	Sun ent. ♋. Longest day.	4 55	7 5		8 4	10 7	
22	Wed	*weather.*	4 55	7 5	♒	9 4	10 43	
23	Thur	*Rain with loud thunder*	4 55	7 5		10 3	11 17	
24	Frid	St. John Baptist.	4 55	7 5	♓	11 25	11 56	
25	Satur	Bish. Gadsden died, '52.	4 55	7 5		11 54	eve 29	
26	S.	Bat. Mechanicsville, '62	4 55	7 5		Morn.	1 26	
27	Mon	Bat. Gaines ville, 1862.	4 56	7 4	♈	0 34	2 19	
28	Tues	♀'s greatest elong'n W	4 56	7 4		1 3	3 20	
29	Wed	Bat. Frazer's Farm, '62	4 56	7 4	♉	1 37	4 30	
30	Thur	Bat. Richmond, 1862.	4 56	7 4		2 8	5 35	

7th Month JULY, 1864 31 days

MOON'S PHASES.	D.	H.	M.	
New Moon	3	6	41	eve.
First Quarter	11	6	43	eve.
Full Moon	19	0	54	mo.
Last Quarter	25	8	1	eve.

EQUATION OF TIME — Sun slow.

D.	1	5	9	13	17	21	25	29
M. S.	3 33	4 16	4 54	5 26	5 50	6 6	6 13	6 10

D of M	D. of W.	Various Phenomena.	Sun rises H. M.	Sun sets H. M.	MOON'S PLACE.	Moon ri. & sets H. M.	High tide Savannah H. M.
1	Frid	Bat. Richmond, 1862.	4 56	7 4	♉	2 43	6 43
2	Satur	*Warm and dry.*	4 56	7 4	♊	3 50	7 45
3	S.	Fort Erie taken, 1814.	4 57	7 3		sets.	8 40
4	Mon	U. S. Dec. Indepen.'76.	4 57	7 3	♋	7 48	9 32
5	Tues	☾ highest.	4 57	7 3		8 31	10 20
6	Wed	☽ in Apogee.	4 58	7 2	♌	9 15	11 4
7	Thur	*Cloudy and some rain.*	4 58	7 2		9 58	11 46
8	Frid	Antares sou 9h 12m.	4 58	7 2	♍	10 42	Morn.
9	Satur	Pres. Taylor died 1850.	4 59	7 1		11 12	0 28
10	S.	Columbus born, 1447.	4 59	7 1	♎	11 57	1 6
11	Mon	John Q Adams b. 1867.	4 59	7 1		morn.	1 54
12	Tues	Altair sou 0h 19m.	5 0	7 0	♏	0 38	2 40
13	Wed	*Sultry and unpleasant*	5 0	7 0		1 12	3 33
14	Thur	☾ ☌ ♃ at 3h 10m morn.	5 1	6 59	♐	1 42	4 31
15	Frid	Antares sou 8h 44m.	5 1	6 59		[illegible] 10	5 42
16	Satur	Moon lowest.	5 2	6 58		2 54	6 44
17	S.	*Cloudy and*	5 2	6 58	♑	3 25	7 40
18	Mon	♀ ☌ Sun Superior.	5 3	6 57		4 21	8 25
19	Tues	Cong. met at Rich'd '61	5 3	6 57	♒	rises.	9 7
20	Wed	Moon in Perigee.	5 4	6 56		8 0	9 46
21	Thur	Bat. Manassas June. '61	5 5	6 55	♓	8 50	10 26
22	Frid	Sun enters ♌.	5 5	6 55		9 31	11 3
23	Satur	*perhaps a fine rain*	5 6	6 54		10 24	11 42
24	S.	Vega sou 10h 20m.	5 6	6 54	♈	11 10	M. 24
25	Mon	St. James. *will fall*	5 7	6 53		morn.	1 8
26	Tues	St. Anne.	5 8	6 52	♉	0 2	1 57
27	Wed	*Warm and unpleasant.*	5 8	6 52		0 42	2 54
28	Thur	Dog days begin.	5 9	6 51		1 12	4 6
29	Frid	Vega sou 10h 0m.	5 10	6 50	♊	2 2	5 15
30	Satur	*Perhaps a storm of rain*	5 11	6 49		2 48	6 30
31	S.	*and hail*	5 11	6 49	♋	3 33	7 37

MOON'S PHASES.				EQUATION OF TIME.

	D.	H.	M.
New Moon	2	9	12	mo.
First Quarter	10	7	28	mo
Full Moon	17	8	2	mo.
Last Quarter	24	5	40	mo.

Sun slow

м.	6	11	33	46	51	49	40
M.	6	5	5	4	3	2	0
D.	1	5	9	13	17	21	25	29

D. of M.	D. of W.	Various Phenomena.	Sun rises H. M.	Sun sets H. M.	Moon's place	Moon ri & sts H. M.	Phila. & Savannah H. M.
1	Mon	America discov. 1492.	5 12	6 48	♋	4 21	8 33
2	Tues	☾ in Apogee. . Rainy	5 13	6 47	♌	Sets.	9 23
3	Wed	Burr's trial com.' 1807.	5 13	6 47		7 40	10 8
4	Thur	Brownstown Bat. 1812.	5 14	6 46	♍	8 25	10 48
5	Frid	Bat Baton Rouge, 1862.	5 15	6 45	.	9 12	11 24
6	Satur	Ship Arkansas dest. '62	5 16	6 44	♎	9 54	11 56
7	S.	Sultry . [men '62	5 17	6 43		10 38	Morn.
8	Mon	Lincoln's call, 600,000	5 17	6 43	♏	11 10	0 36
9	Tues	Bat. Oak Hill, 1861.	5 18	6 42		11 56	1 13
10	Wed	. and dry	5 19	6 41	♐	Morn.	1 53
11	Thur	Lyon's defeat, 1861.	5 20	6 40		0 14	2 34
12	Frid	George IV. born, 1762.	5 21	6 39		1 31	3 35
13	Satur	Moon lowest. weathsr.	5 22	6 38	♑	2 20	4 49
14	S.	Altair sou 10h 9m.	5 22	6 38		3 14	6 2
15	Mon	Bonaparte born, 1769.	5 23	6 37	♒	4 2	7 8
16	Tues	☿ greatest elongation E	5 24	6 36		4 40	8 1
17	Wed	☿ visible in the eve'ng.	5 25	6 35		Rises.	8 45
18	Thur	Moon in Perigee.	5 26	6 34	♓	7 20	9 24
19	Frid	Warm and disagreeable	5 27	6 33		8 2	10 5
20	Satur	Bat. in Mexico, 1847.	5 28	6 32	♈	8 45	10 42
21	S.	Layfayette taken, 1792.	5 29	6 31		9 30	11 23
22	Mon	☽ enters ♍. weather.	5 30	6 30		10 25	Eve.5
23	Tues	A great storm may	5 31	6 29	♉	11 20	0 47
24	Wed	St. Bartholomew. now	5 32	6 28		Morn.	1 39
25	Thur	Bp. Bowen died 1839.	5 33	6 27	♊	0 12	2 20
26	Frid	Dr. Adam Clark d. '32	5 34	6 26		0 58	3 36
27	Satur	Dr. Herschel died, 1822	5 35	6 25		1 42	4 58
28	S.	☽ highest. Le expected.	5 36	6 24	♋	2 30	6 20
29	Mon	Bat. Richmond. Ky. '62	5 37	6 23		3 21	7 36
30	Tues	Battle Manassas, 1862	5 38	6 22	♌	4 2	8 23
31	Wed	Moon in Apogee.	5 39	6 21		4 45	9 14

9th Month SEPTEMBER, 1864 30 days

MOON'S PHASES.

New Moon	1	1	mo.	
First Quarter	8	6 46	eve.	
Full Moon	15	8 43	eve.	
Last Quarter	22	6 0	eve.	
New Moon	30	5 39	eve.	

Sun fast.

EQUATION OF TIME

D. D. of M. W	Various Phenomena.	Sun rises. H.M.	Sun sets. H.M.		PLACE	Moon ri sets M. M.M.	Hi HAVEN AU M.
1 Thur	& Clock agree, Fair	5 39	5 21			sets.	9 50
2 Frid	and mild weather	5 40	6 20			7 0	10 35
3 Satur	☽ ☌ ♄ Ⓞ, Cromwell d.	5 41	8 19			8 50	10 59
4 S.	[1658	5 42	8 18			8 40	11 33
5 Mon	Dog days end.	5 42	5 17	♏		9 27	morn.
6 Tues	Lafayette, born, 1757.	5 44	6 16			10 48	0 16
7 Wed	.	5 45	6 15			11 10	0 56
8 Thur	Bat. Eutaw, 1781. rain	5 46	5 14			morn.	1 12
9 Frid	☽ lowest. with thunder	5 47	6 13			8 24	1 51
10 Satur	Bat. Lake Erie, 1813.	5 48	6 12			0 44	2 44
11 S.	7's rise 6h 5m	5 49	6 14	♒		1 30	3 57
12 Mon	Warm and cloudy.	4 50	6 10			2 35	5 17
13 Tues	Bat. Cotton Hill, '62.	5 51	6 9			8 34	6 53
14 Wed	Moscow burned, 1812.	5 52	6 8	♓		4 35	7 37
15 Thur	Surren. of N. Y., 1776	5 53	6 7			rises.	8 18
16 Frid	Fomalhaut sou. 11h 4m	5 54	6 6	♈		0 40	9 2
17 Satur	Battle Sharpsburg, 62	5 55	6 5			7 31	9 41
18 S.	Stormy and boisterous	5 56	6 4			8 42	10 80
19 Mon	Battle Iuka, 1862.	5 57	6 3	♉		9 15	11 1
20 Tues	Bat. Shepardstown, 62	5 58	6 2			10 6	11 44
21 Wed	St. Matthews.	5 59	6 1	♊		11 10	ev. 27
22 Thur	Days and nights equal	6 0	6 0			moon.	1 18
23 Frid	☉ enters ♎ months.	6 1	5 59			0 4	8 8
24 Satur	☽ highest. may now	6 2	5 58	♋		0 45	3 25
25 S.	be expected	6 3	5 57			1 40	4 46
26 Mon	Gen. Beauregard at	6 4	5 56	♌		2 15	6 10
27 Tues	Charleston, 1863	6 5	5 55			3 2	7 15
28 Wed	Detroit retaken, 1413.	6 6	5 54	♍		3 50	8 8
29 Thur	St. Michael and all ang.	6 7	5 53			4 51	8 49
30 Frid	St. Jerome. Fair and	6 8	5 52			sets.	9 25
	pleasant.						

10th Month OCTOBER, 1864 31 days

MOON'S PHASES.	D.	H.	M.	
First Quarter	8	5	13	mo.
Full Moon	15	0	40	mo.
Last Quarter	22	9	23	mo.
New Moon	30	9	56	mo.

EQUATION OF TIME. Sun fast.

D.	M.	S.
1	10	27
5	11	41
9	12	48
13	13	48
17	14	39
21	15	20
25	15	51
29	16	11

D. of M.	D. of W	Various Phenomena.	Sun rises H.	M.	Sun sets H.	M.	Moon's Place	Moon ri & sts H.	M.	High tide Savannah H.	M.
1	Satur	Moon ☌ ♀ *Cool and*	6	9	5	51	[illegible]	6	31	9	59
2	*S.*	Major Andre exe. 1780.	6	10	5	50	♏	7	10	10	39
3	Mon	Battle Corinth, 1862.	6	11	5	49		7	29	11	1
4	Tues	*pleasant weather.*	6	12	5	48	♐	8	15	11	32
5	Wed	Moon ☌ ♃	6	13	5	47		9	12	Morn.	
6	Thur	Moon lowest *Cloudy*	6	14	5	46	♑	10	25	0	16
7	Frid	Bat King's Mount. '80.	6	15	5	45		11	36	0	36
8	Satur	Battle, Perryville, 1862.	6	15	5	45		morn.		1	16
9	*S.*	Galveston taken, 1862	6	16	5	44	♒	0	25	2	[illegible]
10	Mon	Gen Stuart in Penn. '62	6	17	5	43		1	20	3	16
11	Tues	Moon in Perigee. *and*	6	18	5	42	♓	2	15	4	3[illegible]
12	Wed	*windy weather.*	6	19	5	41		3	8	5	54
13	Thur	Fomalhaut sou 9h 18m.	6	20	5	40		4	46	7	1
14	Frid	♄ ☌ ☉ *Cool mornings*	6	21	5	39	♈	5	20	7	49
15	Satur	Bank Panic, 1857.	6	22	5	38		rises.		8	32
16	*S.*	Raid at Harp. Ferry, '59	6	23	5	37	♉	6	57	9	12
17	Mon	Burgoyne surrend 1777.	6	24	5	36		7	42	9	55
18	Tues	St. Luke.	6	25	5	35		8	3[illegible]	10	40
19	Wed	Cornwallis sur 1781.	6	26	5	34	♊	9	31	11	21
20	Thur	*Now we may expect*	6	27	5	33		10	23	E.	1[illegible]
21	Frid	☾ highest. *frost.*	6	28	5	32	♋	11	25	0	58
22	Satur	Fomalhaut sou 8h 43m.	6	29	5	31		morn.		1	55
23	*S.*	☉ enters ♏ *Cloudy and*	6	30	5	30	♌	0	28	3	4
24	Mon	Moon in Apogee. *windy*	6	31	5	29		1	11	4	27
25	Tues	7 *s sou 1h 41m.	6	32	5	28		2	3	5	49
26	Wed	*Changeable and*	6	33	5	27	♍	2	46	6	55
27	Thur	Fomalhaut sou 8h 23m.	6	34	5	26		3	38	7	44
28	Frid	St. Sim. and St. Jude.	6	35	5	25	♎	4	27	8	25
29	Satur	*unpleasant*	6	36	5	24		5	15	8	59
30	*S.*	Sun eclipsed, invisible,	6	37	5	23	♏	sets.		9	32
31	Mon	7*s sou 1h 0m. *weather.*	6	38	5	22		6	12	10	5

11th Month   NOVEMBER, 1864   30 days

MOON'S PHASES.				Sun fast.	EQUATION OF TIME.
	D.	H.	M		
First Quarter	6	3 35	eve.		a. 10 18 · 15 15 · 9 59 · 29 29 · 46 46 · 49 40 · 20 20
Full Moon	13	11 45	mo.		r. 16 16 · 10 16 · 15 15 · 13 13 · 17 4 · 12 12 · 11 11
Last Quarter	21	3 33	mo.		p. 5 5 · 10 5 · 13 15 · 17 17 · 21 21 · 25 25 · 29 1
New Moon	29	1 33	mo.		

D. of M.	D of W	Various Phenomena.	Sun rises H.M.	Sun sets H.M.	MOON'S PLACE	Moon ri sets H. M. M.	M. Tide SAVAN-NAH. M.
1	Tues	All Saint's day.	6 39	5 21	♐	6 50	10 34
2	Wed	All Souls' day.	6 40	5 20		7 41	11 6
3	Thur	☽ lowest Fair and	6 40	5 20	♑	8 54	11 37
4	Frid	☽ rises 5h 57m	6 41	5 19		10 2	morn.
5	Satur	Battle Warrenton, 1862	6 42	5 18	♒	11 26	0 16
6	S.	Leonard. frosty morn	6 43	5 17	morn.		1 35
7	Mon	Moon in Perigee. ☽ rises	6 44	5 18		0 15	2 34
8	Tues	Rainy and windy	6 45	5 15	♓	1 16	3 53
9	Wed	Tide springs 1h 31m	6 46	5 14		2 21	5 9
10	Thur	Milton died, 1674.	6 46	5 14	♈	3 28	6 21
11	Frid	☽ far south 1h 26m	6 47	5 13		4 36	7 16
12	Satur	· Cool for this month.	6 48	5 12		5 49	8 4
13	S.	Meteor shower, '33 & '37.	6 49	5 11	♉	rises.	8 49
14	Mon	Chas. Carroll d., 1832	6 49	5 11		6 11	9 35
15	Tues	Sirius rises 9h 57m	6 50	5 10	♊	6 58	10 21
16	Wed	Tea dest'd Boston, 1773	6 51	5 9		7 46	11 7
17	Thur	Moon highest. Fair and	6 52	5 8	♋	8 35	11 54
18	Frid	☽ rises 5h 20m mild	6 52	5 8		9 28	eve. 45
19	Satur	7 Stars sou. 11h 1m.	6 53	5 7		10 21	1 38
20	S.	Moon in apogee. weather	6 54	5 6	♌	11 26	2 39
21	Mon	Cloudy and damp	6 54	5 6		morn.	3 58
22	Tues	☉ enters ♐.	6 55	5 5	♍	0 20	5 6
23	Wed	Bomb. Ft. Pickens, '61.	6 56	5 5		1 15	6 15
24	Thur	☽ rises at sunset.	6 56	5 4	♎	2 13	7 11
25	Frid	Frosty and fine	6 57	5 3		3 5	7 54
26	Satur	Q. Isabella died, 1504.	6 58	5 2	♏	3 52	8 38
27	S.	Advent Sunday. weather	6 58	5 2		4 46	9 8
28	Mon	A fine time for gather-	6 59	5 1	♐	5 53	9 42
29	Tues	Moon ☉ ⚹ ing Corn	6 59	5 1		sets.	10 13
30	Wed	St. Andrew's Day.	7 0	5 0	♑	6 25	10 45

12th Month   DECEMBER, 1864   · 31 dyas

MOON'S PHASES.

	D. H. M.	
First Quarter,	6	1 51 mo.
Full Moon,	13	1 17 mo.
Last Quarter,	20	10 50 eve.
New Moon,	28	3 47 eve.

Sun fast.

EQUATION OF TIME.

D. M.	S.
1	10 35
5	8 59
9	7 13
13	5 21
17	3 24
21	1 25
25	slow
29	32

D D / M W	Various Phenomena.	Sun rises H.M.	Sun sets H.M.	Moon's Place	Moon ri.&sts H. M.	High tide av'an'h H. M.
1 Thur	Days 10 hours long.	7 05	0 0	♑	7 28	11 18
2 Frid	7 Stars south 10h 50m.	7 14	59		8 15	11 52
3 Satur	John Brown hung, 1859	7 14	59	♒	9 20	morn.
4 S.	Moon in Perigee Windy	7 24	58	●	10 35	0 31
5 Mon	and cold weather.	7 24	58		11 46	1 15
6 Tues	Van Buren born, 1783.	7 24	58	♓	morn.	2 7
7 Wed	7 Stars south 10h 30m.	7 34	57		0 42	3 9
8 Thur	Theo Sedwick died 1859	7 34	57	♈	1 48	4 25
9 Frid	Father Mathew died, '56	7 34	57		2 53	5 35
10 Satur	Cloudy and damp	7 34	57		4 1	6 42
11 S.	Burnside cross'd Rappa-	7 4	56	♉	5 11	7 38
12 Mon	hannock] Rainy and	7 4	56		6 10	8 27
13 Tues	Bat Fredericksburg, '62	7 4	56	♊	rises.	9 15
14 Wed	unpleasant.	7 4	56	●	6 20	10 9
15 Thur	Frosty, bracing and	7 4	56		7 24	10 57
16 Frid	Gt. Fire N. York, 1835.	7 54	55	♋	8 31	11 42
17 Satur	Bat. Goldsboro', 1862.	7 54	55		9 35	eve.28
18 S.	Moon in Apogee.	7 54	55	♌	10 42	1 19
19 Mon	agreeable weather.	7 54	55		11 50	2 8
20 Tues	Battle Dranesville, 1861	7 54	55	♍	morn.	3 4
21 Wed	Sun ent.♑ Shortest day.	7 54	55		0 45	4 13
22 Thur	Land of Pilgrims, 1620.	7 54	55	♎	1 32	5 18
23 Frid	Sir I. Newton born,1642	7 54	55		2 26	6 24
24 Satur	Sun & clock agree.	7 54	55	♏	3 17	7 26
25 S.	CHRISTMAS DAY. Cloudy	7 54	55		4 15	8 3
26 Mon	St. Stephen. and rainy	7 54	55	♐	5 12	8 45
27 Tues	Bat. Vicksburg '62 Cold	7 44	56		6 6	9 21
28 Wed	Innocents. and windy.	7 44	56	♑	sets.	9 56
29 Thur	7 Stars south 9h 3m.	7 44	56		6 1	10 31
30 Frid	Sun in Perigee.	7 44	56	♒	6 54	11 30
31 Satur	Batt Murfreesboro. 1862	7 44	56		7 56	11 01

REPOSITORY

OF

USEFUL KNOWLEDGE.

CONSTITUTION

OF THE

CONFEDERATE STATES OF AMERICA.

———◆———

WE the people of the Confederate States, each State acting in its sovereign and independent character, in order to form a permanent federal government, establish justice, insure domestic tranquility, and secure the blessings of liberty to ourselves and our posterity—invoking the favor and guidance of Almighty God—do ordain and establish this Constitution for the Confederate States of America.

ARTICLE I.

SECTION I.

All legislative powers herein delegated shall be vested in a Congress of the Confederate States, which shall consist of a Senate and House of Representatives.

SECTION II.

1. The House of Representatives shall be composed of members chosen every second year, by the people of the several States; and the electors in each State shall be citizens of the Confederate States, and have the qualifications requisite for electors of the most numerous branch of the State Legislature; no person of foreign birth not a citizen of the Confederate States, shall be allowed to vote for any officer, civil or political, State or Federal.

2. No person shall be a Representative who shall not have attained the age of twenty-five years and be a citizen of the Confederate States, and who shall not when elected, be an inhabitant of that State in which he shall be chosen.

3. Representatives and Direct Taxes shall be apportioned among the several States, which may be included within this Confederacy, according to their respective numbers, which shall be determined by adding to the whole number of free persons, including those bound to service for a term of years, and including Indians not taxed, three-fifths of all slaves. The actual enumeration shall be made within three years after the first meeting of the Congress of the Confederate States, and within every subsequent term of ten years, in such manner as they shall, by law, direct. The number of Representatives shall not exceed one for every fifty thousand, but each State shall have at least one Representative and until such enumeration shall be made, the State of South Carolina shall be entitled to choose six—the State of Georgia, ten,—the State of Alabama, nine—the State of Florida two—the State of Mississippi, seven—the State of Louisiana, six—and the State of Texas, six.

4. When vacancies happen in the representation from any State the Executive authority thereof shall issue writs of election to fill such vacancies.

5. The House of Representatives shall choose their Speaker and other officers, and shall have the sole power of impeachment; except that any judicial or other federal officers resident and acting solely within the limits of any State, may be impeached by a vote of two-thirds of both branches of the Legislature thereof.

SECTION III.

1. The Senate of the Confederate States shall be composed of two Senators from each State, chosen for six years by the Legislature thereof, at the regular session next immediately preceding the commencement of the term of service; and each Senator shall have one vote.

2. Immediately after they shall be assembled, in consequence of the first election, they shall be divided as equally as possible into three classes. The seats of the Senators of the first class shall be vacated at the expiration of the second year; of the second class at the expiration of the fourth year; and of the third class, at the expiration of the sixth year; so that one-third may be chosen every second year; and if vacancies happen by resignation, or otherwise, during the recess of the Legislature of any State, the Executive thereof may make temporary appointments until the next meeting of the Legislature, which shall then fill such vacancies.

3 No person shall be a Senator who shall not have attained the age of thirty years; and be a citizen of the Confederate States; and who shall not when elected, be an inhabitant of the State for which he shall be chosen.

4 The Vice President of the Confederate States shall be President of the Senate, but shall have no vote, unless they shall be equally divided.

5. The Senate shall choose their other officers; and also a President pro tempore in the absence of the Vice President, or when he shall exercise the office of President of the Confederate States.

6. The Senate shall have the sole power to try all impeachments. When sitting for that purpose, they shall be on oath or affirmation. When the President of the Confederate States is tried, the Chief Justice shall preside; and no person shall be convicted without the concurrence of two thirds of the members present.

7. Judgment in cases of impeachment shall not extend farther than to removal from office, and disqualification to hold and enjoy any office of honor or profit, under the Confederate States; but the party convicted shall nevertheless, be liable and subject to indictment, trial, judgment, and punishment according to law.

SECTION IV.

1. The time, place, and manner of holding elections for Senators and Representatives shall be prescribed in each State by the Legislature thereof, subject to the provisions of this Constitution; but the Congress may, at any time, by law, make or alter such regulations, except as to the times and places of choosing Senators.

2. The Congress shall assemble at least once in every year, and such meeting shall be on the first Monday in December, unless they shall, by law, appoint a different day.

SECTION V.

1. Each House shall be the judge of the elections, returns and qualifications of its own members, and a majority of each shall constitute a quorum to do business; but a smaller number may adjourn from day to day, and may be authorized to compel the attendance of absent members, in such manner and under such penalties as each House may provide.

2. Each House may determine the rule of its proceedings, punish its members for disorderly behavior, and with the concurrence of two-thirds of the whole number, expel a member.

3. Each House shall keep a journal of its proceedings, and from time to time publish the same, excepting such parts as may, in their judgment, require secrecy; and the yeas and nays of the members of either House, on any question, shall, at the desire of one-fifth of those present, be entered on the journal.

4. Neither House, during the session of Congress, shall, without the consent of the other, adjourn for more than three days, nor to any other place than that in which the two Houses shall be sitting.

SECTION. VI.

1. The Senators and Representatives shall receive a compensation for their services, to be ascertained by law, and paid out of the Treasury of the Confederate States. They shall, in all cases, except treason, and breach of the peace, be privileged from arrest during their attendance at the session of their respective Houses, and in going to and returning from the same; and for any speech, or debate in either House, they shall not be questioned in any other place.

2. No Senator or Representative shall, during the time for which he was elected, be appointed to any civil office under the authority of the Confederate States, which shall have been created, or the emoluments thereof shall have been increased during such time; and no person holding any office under the Confederate States shall be a member of either House during his continuance in office. But Congress may, by law, grant to the principal officer in each of the Executive Departments a seat upon the floor of either House with the privilege of discussing any measure appertaining to his department.

SECTION VII.

1. All bills for raising revenue shall originate in the House of Representatives; but the Senate may propose or concur with amendments, as on other bills.

2. Every bill which shall have passed both Houses, shall, before it becomes a law, be presented to the President of the Confederate States; if he approve he shall sign it; but if not, he shall return it, with his objections to the House in which it shall have originated, who shall enter the objections at large on their journals, and proceed to reconsider it. If, after such reconsideration, two-thirds of that House shall agree to pass the bill, it shall be sent, together with the objections, to the other House, by which it shall likewise be reconsidered; and if approved by two-thirds of that House, it shall become a law. But in all such cases, the votes of both Houses shall be determined by yeas and nays, and the persons voting for or against the bill shall be entered on the Journal of each House respectively. If any bill shall not be returned by the President within ten days (Sundays excepted) after it shall have been presented to him, the same shall be a law in like manner as if he had signed it, unless the Congress shall, by their adjournment, prevent its return; in which case it shall not be a law. The President may approve any appropriation, and disapprove any other appropriation in the same bill. In such case, he shall, in signing the bill designate the appropriation disapproved; and shall return a copy of such appropriations, with his objections, to the House in which the bill shall have originated and the same proceedings shall then be had as in case of other bills disapproved by the President.

3. Every order, resolution or vote, to which the concurrence of both Houses may be necessary, (except on a question of adjournment) shall be presented to the President of the Confederate States; and before the same shall take effect, shall be approved by him; or being disapproved by him may be repassed by two-thirds of both Houses, according to the rules and limitations prescribed in case of a bill.

SECTION VIII.

The Congress shall have power—

1. To lay and collect taxes, duties, imposts and excises, for revenue necessary to pay the debts, provide for the common defence and carry on the Government of the Confederate States; but no bounties shall be granted from the treasury; nor shall any duties, or taxes on importations from foreign nations be laid to promote or foster any branch of industry; and all duties, imposts and excises shall be uniform throughout the Confederate States:

2. To borrow money on the credit of the Confederate States:

3. To regulate commerce with foreign nations, and among the several States, and with the Indian tribes; but neither this, nor any other clause contained in the Constitution shall ever be construed to delegate the power to Congress to appropriate money for, any internal improvement intended to facilitate commerce, except for the purpose of furnishing lights, beacons and buoys, and other aids to navigation upon the coast, and the improvement of harbors, and the removing of obstructions in river navigation, in all which cases, such duties shall be laid on the navigation facilitated thereby, as may be necessary to pay the costs and expenses thereof:

4. To establish uniform laws of naturalization, and uniform laws on the subject of bankruptcies, throughout the Confederate States: but no law of Congress shall discharge any debt contracted before the passage of the same:

5. To coin money, regulate the value thereof, and of foreign coin, and fix the standard of weights and measures:

6. To provide for the punishment of counterfeiting the securities and current coin of the Confederate States:

7. To establish post offices and post routes; but the expenses of the Post-office Department, after the first day of March, in the year of our Lord, eighteen hundred and sixty three, shall be paid out of its own revenues:

8. To promote the progress of science and useful arts, by securing for limited times to authors and inventors the exclusive right to their respective writings and discoveries:

9. To constitute tribunals inferior to the Supreme Court:

10. To define and punish piracies and felonies committed on the high seas and offences against the law of nations.

11. To declare war, grant letters of marque and reprisal; and make rules concerning captures on land and water.

12. To raise and support armies; but no appropriation of money to that use shall be for a longer term than two years.

13. To provide and maintain a navy.

14. To make rules for government and the regulation of the land and naval forces.

15. To provide for calling forth the militia to execute the laws of the Confederate States, suppress insurrections and repel invasions.

16. To provide for organizing, arming and disciplining the militia, and for governing such part of them as may be employed in the service of the Confederate States; reserving to the States, respectively, the appointment of the officers, and the authority of training the militia according to the discipline prescribed by Congress.

17. To exercise exclusive legislation, in all cases whatsoever, over such district (not exceeding ten miles square) as may, by cession of one or more States, and the acceptance of Congress, become the seat of the Government of the Confederate States; and to exercise like authority over all the places purchased by the consent of the legislature of the State in which the same shall be, for the erection of forts, magazines, arsenals, dockyards, and other needful buildings; and

18. To make all laws which shall be necessary and proper for carrying into execution the foregoing powers, and all other powers vested by this Constitution in the Government of the Confederate States, or in any department or office thereof.

SECTION IX.

1. The importation of negroes of the African race, from any foreign country, other than the slaveholding States or Territories of the United States of America, is hereby forbidden; and Congress is required to pass such laws as shall effectually prevent the same.

2. Congress shall also have power to prohibit the introduction of slaves from any State not a member of, or Territory not belonging to, this Confederacy.

3. The privilege of the writ of habeas corpus shall not be suspended, unless when, in cases of rebellion, or invasion, the public safety may require it.

4. No bill of attainder, or ex post facto law, or law denying or impairing the right of property in negro slaves, shall be passed.

5. No capitation or other direct tax shall be laid, unless in proportion to the census or enumeration hereinbefore directed to be taken.

6. No tax or duty shall be laid on articles exported from any State, except by a vote of two-thirds of both Houses.

7 No preference shall be given by any regulation of commerce or revenue to the ports of one State over those of another.

8 No money shall be drawn from the Treasury, but in consequence of appropriations made by law, and a regular statement and account of the receipts and expenditures of all public money shall be published from time to time.

9. Congress shall appropriate no money from the Treasury, except by a vote of two-thirds of both houses, taken by yeas and nays, unless it be asked and estimated for by some one of the heads of the Department, and submitted to Congress by the President; or for the purpose of paying its own expenses and contingencies; or for the payment of claims against the Confederate States, the justice of which shall have been judicially declared by a tribunal for the investigation of claims against the Government, which it is hereby made the duty of Congress to establish.

10. All bills appropriating money shall specify in Federal currency the exact amount of each appropriation, and the purposes for which it is made; and Congress shall grant no extra compensation to any public contractor, officer, agent or servant, after such contract shall have been made, or such service rendered.

11. No title of nobility shall be granted by the Confederate States; and no person holding any office of profit or trust under them, shall, without the consent of the Congress, accept of any present, emoluments. office, or titles of any kind whatever, from any king, prince, or foreign State.

12. Congress shall make no law respecting an establishment of religion, or prohibiting the free exercise thereof: or abridging the freedom of speech or of the press; or the right of the people peaceably to assemble and petition the Government for a redress of grievances.

13. A well regulated militia being necessary to the security of a free State, the right of the people to keep and bear arms shall not be infringed.

14 No soldier shall, in time of peace, be quartered in any house without the consent of the owner; nor in time of war, but in a manner to be prescribed by law.

15. The right of the people to be secure in their persons, houses, papers, and effects, against unreasonable searches and seizures, shall not be violated; and no warrant shall issue but upon probable cause, supported by oath or affirmation, and particularly describing the place to be searched, and the person or things to be seized.

16. No person shall be held to answer for a capital or otherwise infamous crime, unless on a presentment or indictment of a grand jury, except in cases arising in the land or naval forces, or in the militia, when in actual service, in time of war or public danger; nor shall any person be subject for the same offence to be twice put in jeopardy of life or limb; nor be compelled, in any criminal case, to be a witness against himself; nor be deprived of

life, liberty or property, without due process of law ; nor shall private property be taken for public use, without just compensation.

17. In all criminal prosecutions the accused shall enjoy the right to a speedy and public trial, by an impartial jury of the State and district wherein the crime shall have been committed, which district shall have been previously ascertained by law, and to be informed of the nature and cause of the accusation ; to be confronted with the witnesses against him; to have compulsory process for obtaining witnesses in his favor ; and to have the assistance of counsel for his defence.

18. In suits at common law where the value in controversy shall exceed twenty dollars, the right of trial by jury shall be preserved ; and no fact so tried by a jury shall be otherwise re examined in any court of the Confederacy, than according to the rules of the common law.

19. Excessive bail shall not be required, nor excessive fines be imposed, nor cruel and unjust punishments be inflicted.

20. Every law, or resolution having the force of law, shall relate to but one subject, and that shall be expressed in the title.

SECTION X.

1. No State shall enter into any treaty, alliance, or confederation ; grant letters of marque and reprisal ; coin money, make anything but gold and silver coin a tender in payment of debts ; pass any bill of attainder, or ex post facto law or law, impairing the obligation of contracts ; or grant any title of nobility.

2. No State shall, without the consent of Congress, lay any imposts, or duties on imports or exports, except what may be absolutely necessary for executing its inspection laws ; and the net produce of all duties and imposts laid by any State on imports or exports, shall be for the use of the treasury of the Confederate States ; and all such laws shall be subject to the revision and control of Congress.

3. No State shall without the consent of Congress, lay any duty of tonnage, except on sea-going vessels, for the improvement of its rivers and harbors navigated by the said vessel's ; but such duties shall not conflict with any treaties of the Confederate States with foreign nations ; and any surplus or revenue thus derived, shall, after making such improvements, be paid into the common treasury ; nor shall any State keep troops or ships of war in time of peace, enter into any agreement or compact with another State, or with a foreign power, or engage in war, unless actually invaded, or in such imminent danger as will not admit of delay. But when any river divides or flows through two or more States, they may enter into compacts with each other to improve the navigation thereof.

ARTICLE II.

SECTION I.

1. The executive power shall be vested in a President of the Confederate States of America. He and the Vice-President shall hold their offices for the term of six years, but the President shall not be re-eligible. The President and Vice-President shall be elected as follows :

2. Each State shall appoint, in such manner as the Legislature thereof may direct, a number of electors equal to the whole number of Senators and Representatives to which the State may be entitled in the Congress, but no Senator or Representative, or person holding any office of trust or profit under the Confederate States shall be appointed an elector.

3. The electors shall meet in their respective States and vote by ballot for President and Vice-President, one of whom, at least, shall not be an inhabitant of the same State with themselves ; they shall name in their ballots the persons voted for as President, and in distinct ballots the person voted for as Vice-President, and they shall make distinct lists of all persons voted for as President, and of all persons voted for as Vice President, and

of the number of votes for each, which list they shall sign and certify, and transmit, sealed, to the government of the Confederate States, directed to the President of the Senate ; the President of the Senate shall in the presence of the Senate and House of Representatives, open all the certificates, and the vote shall then be counted ; the person having the greatest number of votes for President shall be the President, if such number be a majority of the whole number of electors appointed ; and if no person have such majority, then from the persons having the highest numbers, not exceeding three, on the list of those voted for as President, the House of Representatives shall choose immediately, by ballot, the President. But in choosing the President, the vote shall be taken by States, the representation from each State having one vote : a quorum for this purpose shall consist of a member or members from two-thirds of the States, and a majority of all the States shall be necessary to a choice. And if the House of Representatives shall not choose a President, whenever the right of choice shall devolve upon them, before the fourth day of March next following, then the Vice-President shall act as President, as in case of the death or other Constitutional disability of the President.

4. The person having the greatest number of votes as Vice-President shall be the Vice-President, if such number be a majority of the whole number of electors appointed, and if no person have a majority, then from the two highest numbers on the list the Senate shall, choose the Vice-President ; a quorum for the purpose shall consist of two thirds of the whole number of Senators, and a majority of the whole number shall be necessary to a choice.

5. No person constitutionally ineligible to the office of President shall be eligible to that of Vice-President of the Confederate State.

6. The Congress may determine the time of choosing the electors, and the day on which they shall give their votes ; which day shall be the same throughout the Confederate States.

7. No person except a natural born citizen of the Confederate States, or a citizen thereof, at the time of the adoption of the Constitution, or a citizen thereof born in the United States prior to the 20th of December, 1860, shall be eligible to the office of President ; neither shall any person be eligible to that office who shall not have attained the age of thirty-five years, and been fourteen years a resident within the limits of the Confederate States as they may exist at the time of his election.

8. In case of the removal of the President from office, or of his death, re-, ignation, or inability to discharge the powers and duties of the said office, the same shall devolve on the Vice-President ; and the Congress may, by law, provide for the case of removal, death, resignation or inability, both as the President and Vice-President, declaring what officer shall then act as President, and such officer shall act accordingly until the disability be removed or a President shall be elected.

9. The President shall, at stated times, receive for his services a compensation which shall neither be increased nor diminished during the period for which he shall have been elected ; and he shall not receive within that period any other emolument from the Confederate States, or any of them.

10. Before he enters on the execution of his office, he shall take the following oath or affirmation :
"I do solemnly swear—or affirm—that I will faithfully execute the office of President of the Confederate States, and will, to the best of my ability, preserve, protect and defend the Constitution thereof."

SECTION II.

1. The President shall be Commander-in-Chief of the army and navy of the Confederate States, and of the militia of the several States, when called into the actual service of the Confederate States ; he may require the opinion, in writing, of the principal officer in each of the Executive Departments,

upon any subject, relating to the duties of their respective offices; and he shall have power to grant reprieves and pardons for offences against the Confederate States, except in cases of impeachment.

2. He shall have power, by and with the advice and consent of the Senate, to make treaties, provided two thirds of the Senators present concur, and he shall nominate, and by and with the advice and consent of the Senate, shall appoint ambassadors, other public ministers and consuls, Judges of the Supreme Court, and all other officers of the Confederate States, whose appointments are not herein otherwise provided for, and which shall be established by law; but the Congress may, by law, vest the appointment of such inferior officers, as they think proper, in the President alone, in the Courts of Law, or in the heads of Departments.

3. The principal in each of the Executive Departments, and all persons connected with the diplomatic service, may be removed from office at the pleasure of the President. All other civil officers of the Executive Department may be removed at any time by the President, or other appointing power, when their services are u necessary, or for dishonesty, incapacity, in efficiency, misconduct, or neglect or duty , and when so removed, the removal shall be reported to the Senate together with the reasons therefor.

4. The President shall have power to fill all vacancies that may happen during the recess of the Senate by granting commissions which shall expire at the end of their next session : but no person rejected by the Senate shall be re-appointed to the same office during their ensuing recess.

SECTION III.

1. The President shall, from time to time, give to the Congress information of the state of the Confederacy, and recommend to their consideration such measures as he shall judge necessary and expedient ; he may, on extraordinary occasions, convene both Houses, or either of them ; and in case of disagreement between them, with respect to the time of adjournment he may adjourn them to such time as he shall think proper ; he shall receive ambassadors and other public ministers ; he shall take care that the laws be faithfully executed, and shall commission all the officers of the Confederate States.

SECTION IV.

1. The President, Vice President, and all civil officers of the Confederate States, shall be removed from office on impeachment for, and conviction of treason, bribery, or other high crimes and misdemeanors.

ARTICLE III.

SECTION I.

1. The judicial power of the Confederate States shall be vested in one Superior Court, and in such Inferior Courts as the Congress may from time to time order and establish. The judges, both of the Superior and Inferior Courts, shall hold their offices during good behavior, and shall, at stated times, receive for their services a compensation, which shall not be diminished during their continuance in office.

SECTION II.

1. The judicial power shall extend to all cases arising under this Constitution the laws of the Confederate States, and treaties made, or which shall be made, under their authority ; to all cases affecting ambassadors, other public ministers and consuls ; to all cases of admiralty and maritime jurisdiction ; to controversies to which the Confederate States shall be a party ; to controversies between two or more States ; between a State and citizens of another State, where the State is plaintiff; between citizens claiming

lauds under grants from different States ; and between the State or the
citizens thereof, and foreign States, citizens or subjects ; but no State shall
be sued by a citizen or subject of any foreign State.

2. In all cases affecting ambassadors, other public ministers, and consuls,
and those in which a State shall be a party, the Supreme Court shall have
original jurisdiction. In all other cases before-mentioned, the Supreme
Court shall have appellate jurisdiction, both as to law and facts, with such
exceptions and under such regulations as the Congress shall make.

3. The trial of all crimes, except in cases of impeachment, shall be by
jury, and such trial shall be held in the State where the said crime shall
have been committed ; but when not committed within any State, the trial
shall be at such place or places as the Congress may by law have directed.

SECTION III.

1. Treason against the Confederate States shall consist only in levying
war against them, or in adhering to their enemies, giving them aid and
comfort. No person shall be convicted of treason, unless on the testimony
of two witnesses to the same overt act, or on confession in open court.

2. The Congress shall have power to declare the punishment of treason,
but no attainder of treason shall work corruption of blood, or forfeiture,
except during the life of the person attainted.

ARTICLE IV.

SECTION I.

1. Full faith and credit shall be given in each State to the public acts,
records and judicial proceedings of every other State. And the Congress
may, by general laws, prescribe the manner in which such acts, records
and proceedings shall be proved, and the effect thereof.

SECTION II.

1. The citizens of each State shall be entitled to all the privileges and
immunities of citizens in the several States, and shall have the right of
transit and sojourn in any State of the Confederacy, with their slaves and
other property ; and the right of property in said slaves shall not be thereby
impaired.

2. A person charged in any State with treason, felony, or other crime
against the law of such State, shall, on the demand of the Executive authority of the State from which he fled, be delivered up to be removed to
the State having jurisdiction of the crime.

3. No slave, or other person held to service or labor, in any State or Territory of the Confederate States, under the laws thereof, escaping or lawfully
carried into another, shall, in consequence of any law or regulation therein,
be discharged from such service or labor ; but shall be delivered up on claim
of the party to whom such slave belongs, or to whom such labor or service
may be due.

SECTION III.

1. Other States may be admitted into this Confederacy by a vote of two-
thirds of the whole House of Representatives, and two-thirds of the Senate,
the Senate voting by States ; but no new State shall be formed or erected
within the jurisdiction of any other State ; nor any State be formed by the
junction of two or more States, or parts of States, without the consent of the
Legislatures of the States concerned, as well as of the Congress.

2. The Congress shall have power to dispose of and make all needful
rules and regulations concerning the property of the Confederate States, including the lands thereof.

3. The Confederate States may acquire new territory ; and Congress shall have power to legislate and provide governments for the inhabitants of all territory belonging to the Confederate States, lying without the limits of the several States ; and may permit them, at such times, and in such manner, as it may by law provide, to form States to be admitted into the Confederacy. In all such territory, the institution of negro slavery, as it now exists in the Confederate States, shall be recognized and protected by Congress, and by the Territorial Government ; and the inhabitants of the several Confederate States and Territories shall have the right to take to such Territory any slaves, lawfully held by them in any of the States or Territories of the Confederate States.

4. The Confederate States shall guarantee to every State that is or hereafter may become a member of this Confederacy, a republican form of government, and shall protect each of them against invasion ; and on application of the Legislature, (or of the Executive, when the Legislature is in session.) against domestic violence.

ARTICLE V.

SECTION 1.

1. Upon the demand of any three States, legally assembled in their several conventions, the Congress shall summon a convention of all the States, to take into consideration such amendments to the Constitution as the said States all concur in suggesting at the time when the said demand is made ; and should any of the proposed amendments to the Constitution be agreed on by the said convention—voting by States—and the same be ratified by the Legislatures of two-thirds of the several States, or by conventions in two-thirds thereof—as the one or the other mode of ratification may be proposed by the general convention—they shall thenceforward form a part of this Constitution. But no State shall, without its consent, be deprived of its equal representation in the Senate.

ARTICLE VI.

1. The Government established by this Constitution is the successor of the Provisional Government of the Confederate States of America, and all the laws passed by the latter shall continue in force until the same shall be repealed or modified ; and all the officers appointed by the same shall remain in office until their successors are appointed and qualified, or the offices abolished.

2. All debts contracted, and engagements entered into, before the adoption of this Constitution, shall be as valid against the Confederate States under this Constitution as under the Provisional Government.

3. This Constitution and the laws of the Confederate States, made in pursuance thereof, and all treaties made, or which shall be made, under the authority of the Confederate States, shall be the supreme law of the land ; and the judges in every State shall be bound thereby, anything in the Constitution or laws of any State to the contrary notwithstanding.

4. The Senators and Representatives before mentioned, and the members of the several State Legislatures, and all executive and judicial officers, both of the Confederate States and of the several States, shall be bound by oath or affirmation to support this Constitution ; but no religious test shall ever be required as a qualification to any office of public trust under the Confederate States.

5. The enumeration, in the Constitution, of certain rights shall not be construed to deny or disparage others retained by the people of the several States.

6. The powers not delegated to the Confederate States by the Constitution, nor prohibited by it to the States, are reserved to the States, respectively, or to the people thereof.

ARTICLE VII.

1. The ratification of the Convention of five States shall be sufficient for the establishment of this Constitution between the States so ratifying the same.

2 When five States shall have ratified this Constitution in the manner before specified, the Congress under the Provisional Constitution shall prescribe the time for holding the election of President and Vice-President, and for the meeting of the Electoral College, and for counting the votes, and inaugurating the President. They shall, also, prescribe the time for holding the first election of members of Congress under this Constitution, and the time for assembling the same. Until the assembling of such Congress the Congress under the provisional constitution shall continue to exercise the legislative powers granted them : not extending beyond the time limited by the Constitution of the Provisional Government.

Adopted, unanimously, March 11, 1861.

Note.—The Constitution of the Southern Confederation differs from that of the Union mainly in the following points. The Southern Constitution absolutely prohibits the ovy sea slave trade ; that of the Union does not. It permits Cabinet Ministers to take part in the di cussions of Congress. It prohibits bounties or duties to foster any branch of industry. After a specified time the post-office must cover its own expenses. No extra compensation to be paid to any contractor. Log-rolling is prohibited. The President is to hold office for six years, and is not to be re-eligible. The subordinate government officers not to be removed by the President without a report to the Senate, giving his reasons.

It will be observed that these alterations remove several of the grossest evils described as resulting from the institutions of the Union. The special clauses referring to the post office and to contractors, are intended to remove notorious sources of corruption heretofore in active operation.

Curious Facts.—According to the American Encyclopedia, the number of languages spoken is 4,164. The number of men is about equal to the number of women. The average of human life is thirty-three years. One quarter die before the age of seventeen. To every one thousand persons, only one reaches one hundred years. To every one hundred, only six reaches seventy-five years ; and not more than one in five hundred will reach eighty years. There are one thousand million of inhabitants. Of these 33,333,883 die every year ; 91,824 die every day ; 7,780 every hour and 60 every minute, or one every second. These losses are about balanced by an equal number of births. The married are longer-lived than the single, and above all, those who observe a sober and industrious conduct. Tall men live longer than short ones. Women have more chances of life previous to the age of fifty years than men, but fewer after. The number of marriages is in the proportion of seventy-six to one hundred. Marriages are more frequent after the equinoxes —that is during the month of June and December. Those born in the spring are generally more robust than others. Births and deaths are more frequent by night than by day.

STATE GOVERNMENTS OF THE CONFEDERATE STATES.

States	Capitals.	Governors.	Term Expires.	Salary.	Legislature Meets.	General Election.
Alabama,	Montgomery.	T. H. Watts.	December, 1865.	$4,000	2d Monday Nov.	1st Monday Aug.
Arkansas,	Little Rock.	H. Flanagan.	November, 1864.	2500	1st Monday Nov.	1st Thurs. Sept.
Georgia,	Milledgeville	Jos. E. Brown.	November, 1863.	4000	1st Monday Nov	1st Monday Oct.
Louisiana,	Shreveport.	Thos. O. Moore.	January, 1864.	4000	3d Monday Nov	1st Monday N. v.
Mississippi,	Macon.	J. J. Pettus.	November, 1863.	400k	1st Monday Nov.	1st Monday Oct.
North Carolina,	Raleigh.	Z. B. Vance.	January, 1864.	3500	3d Monday Nov.	1st Thurs. Aug.
South Carolina,	Columbia.	M. L. Bonham.	December, 1864	3500	4th Monday Nov.	2d Monday Oct.
Tennessee,		L. G. Harris.	October, 1863.	3000	1st Monday Oct.	1st Thurs. Aug.
Texas, —	Austin.	P. Murrah.	December, 1866	3000	1st Monday Nov.	1st Monday Aug.
Virginia,	Richmond.	Wm. Smith.	January, 1866.	5000	1st Monday Dec.	4th Thurs. Aug.
Florida,	Tallahassee.	John Milton.	October, 1865.	2500	1st Monday Nov.	1st Monday Oct.
Missouri,		T. C. Reynolds.	December, 1864	3500	4th Mond'y Nov.	1st Monday Aug.
Kentucky,		R. Hawes.			1st December.	1st Monday Aug.

DATES OF SECESSION OF THE SOUTHERN STATES FROM THE UNION.

South Carolina seceded,	December 20th, 1860
Mississippi,	January 9th, 1861
Florida,	January 10, 1861
Alabama,	January 11, 1861
Georgia,	January 19, 1861
Louisiana,	January 25, 1861
Texas,	February 1, 1861
Virginia,	April 17, 1861
Tennessee,	May 6, 1861
Arkansas,	May 6, 1861
North Carolina,	May 20, 1861
Missouri,	October 28, 1861
Kentucky,	November 19, 1861

CONFEDERATE STATES.

The organization of the Confederate States Government commenced under a Provisional Constitution on the 8th day of February, 1861, and expired on the 18th day of February, 1862. Jefferson Davis, of Mississippi, and Alexander H. Stephens, of Georgia, were chosen as President and Vice President for the Provisional term of one year.

The first Presidential term of six years under the permanent Constitution commenced on the 18th February, 1862, and will expire on the 18th day of February, 1868.

The first election for President and Vice President under the permanent Constitution took place on the 6th day of November, 1861, in each State of the Confederacy.

Total number of States voting, 11.

Total number of electoral votes cast, 109.

Of which number, Jefferson Davis, of Mississippi, received for the office of President of the Confederate States, 109.

Alexander H. Stephens, of Georgia, received for the office of Vice President of the Confederate States, 109.

The number of electoral votes cast by the several States is as follows :

	Representation in Congress.	Votes.
Virginia	16	18
North Carolina	10	12
South Carolina	6	8
Georgia	10	10
Florida	9	4
Alabama	9	11
Louisiana	6	8
Texas	6	8
Arkansas	4	6
Mississippi	7	9
Tennessee	11	13
	87	109

SALARIES OF THE EXECUTIVE OFFICERS.

President,	$25.000 per year.
Vice-President,	6.000 "
Secretary of State,	6,000 "
" Treasury,	6,000 "
" War,	6,000 "
" Navy,	6,000 "
Attorney General,	6,000 "
Postmaster-General,	6,000 "

The salary of members of Congress shall be eight dollars per day during the session. Each member shall be allowed ten cents per mile for coming to, and ten cents for returning from, the place where Congress may assemble for each session. The salary of the President of Congress shall be sixteen dollars per day, and the mileage the same as members.

The President and Vice-President are elected for a term of six years, and are not re-eligible to office. The Senate is composed of two members from each State in the Confederacy, chosen by the legislatures of each State, for six years. The Senate is divided into three classes, and one-third of their number are chosen every two years. The members of the House of Representatives are elected by the people for a term of two years. Congress assembles once in every year, commencing on the 18th day of February.

GOVERNMENT OF THE CONFEDERATE STATES.

(Capital located at Richmond, Va.)

Jefferson Davis, of Mississippi, President,
Alexander H. Stephens, of Georgia, Vice-President,

The Cabinet.

J. P. Benjamin, of Louisiana, Secretary of State,
C. G. Memminger, of South Carolina, Secretary of Treasury.
James A. Seddon, of Virginia, Secretary of War.
S. R. Mallory, of Florida, Secretary of Navy.
Thomas H. Watts, of Alabama, Attorney-General.
J. H. Reagan, of Texas, Postmaster-General.

HEADS OF DEPARTMENTS.

Rufus R. Rhodes, of Mississippi, Commissioner of Patents.
G. E. W. Nelson, Superintendent of Public Printing.
Gen. S. Cooper. Adjutant and Inspector General.
Col. John S. Preston, Chief of Bureau of Conscription.
Brig. Gen. A. R. Lawton, Quartermaster General.
L. B. Northup, Commissary-General.
S. P Moore, Surgeon General.
E. W. Johns, Medical Purveyor.

FIRST CONGRESS OF THE CONFEDERATE STATES.

Senate.

Alabama--†Clement C. Clay, Robert Jemison, Jr.
Arkansas—†Robt. W. Johnson, Charles B. Mitchell.
Florida—James M. Baker, †Augustus E. Maxwell.
Georgia —Benjamin H. Hill, Herschel V. Johnson.
Kentucky—†Henry C. Burnett, †William E. Simms.
Louisiana - Thomas J. Semmes, Edward Sparrow,
Mississippi—†Albert G. Brown, James Phelan.
Missouri -†John B. Clark, R. S. T. Peyton.
North Carolina—George Davis. William T. Dortch.
South Carolina—†Robt. W. Barnwell, †James L. Orr.
Tennessee—Langdon C. Haynes, Gustavus A. Henry.
Texas—William S. Oldham. †Louis T. Wigfall.
Virginia—Robert M. O. T. Hunter, Allen T. Caperton.

Those having the † prefixed have served in the United States Congress. The number of old Congressmen in the Senate will be twelve. New Congressmen, fourteen. Total, twenty-six.

House of Representatives.

Dist. **ALABAMA.**
1. Thomas J. Foster.
2. †William R Smith.
3. W. R. W. Cobb.
4. M. N. Cruikshank.
5. Francis S. Lyon.
6. Wm. P. Chilton.
7. †David Clopton.
8. †James L. Pugh.
9. J. S. Dickinson.

ARKANSAS.
1. Felix I. Batson.
2. Grandison D. Royston.
3. Augustus H. Garland.
4. Thomas B. Hanly.

FLORIDA.
1. James B. Dawkins.
2. Robert B. Hilton.

Dist. **GEORGIA.**
1. Julian Hartridge.
2. C. J. Munnerlyn.
3. Hines Holt.
4. Augustus H. Kenan.
5. David W. Lewis.
6. William W. Clark.
7. †Robert P. Trippe.
8. †Lucius J. Gartrell.
9. Hardy Strickland.
10. †Augustus R. Wright.

LOUISIANA.
1. Charles J. Villiere.
2. †Charles M. Conrad.
3. Duncan F. Keener.
4. Lucien J. Dupre.
5. John F. Lewis.
6. John Perkins, Jr.

Dist	KENTUCKY.	Dist	SOUTH CAROLINA.
1.	Alfred Boyd.	1. ‡John. McQueen.	
2.	John W. Crockett.	2. W. Porcher Miles.	
3.	H. E. Read.	3. L. M. Ayer.	
4.	Geo. W. Ewing.	4. ‡Milledge L. Bonham.	
5.	‡James S. Chrisman.	5. James Farrow.	
6.	T. L. Burnett.	6. Wm. W. Boyce.	

TENNESSEE.
7. H. W. Bruce,
8. S. S. Scott.	1. Joseph T. Heiskell.
9. E. M. Bruce.	2. Wm. G. Swan.
10. J. W. Moore.	3. W. H. Tebbs.
11. Robt. J. Breckinridge.	4. E. L. Gardenshire.
12. John M. Elliott.	5. ‡Henry S. Foote.
	6. ‡Meredith P Gentry.
MISSISSIPPI.	7. ‡George W. Jones.
1. J. W. Clapp.	8. Thomas Meneese.
2. ‡Reuben Davis.	9. ‡J. D. C. Atkins.
3. Israel Welch.	10. John V. Wright.
4. H. C. Chambers.	11. David M. Currin.
5. ‡O. R. Singleton.	TEXAS.
6 E. Barksdale.	1. ‡John A. Wilcox.
7. ‡John J. McRae.	2. G. C. Herbert.
	3. Peter W. Gray.
MISSOURI.	4. B. F. Sexton.
1. W. M. Cook.	5. M. D. Graham.
2. Thomas A. Harris.	6. Wm. B. Wright.
3. Casper W Bell,	VIRGINIA.
4. A. H. Conrow.	1. Robt. L. Montague.
5. George G. Vest.	2. Robt. H. Whitfield.
6. Thomas W. Freeman.	3. William C. Wickham,
7. John Hyer.	4. Thos. S. Gholson.
	5. ‡Thomas S. Bocock.
NORTH CAROLINA.	6. John Goode, Jr.
1. ‡W. N. H. Smith,	7. Wm. C. Rives.
2. Robert R. Bridgers.	8. ‡Daniel G. DeJarnette.
3. Owen R. Keenan.	9. David Funsten.
4. T. D. McDowell.	10. F. W. M. Holliday.
5. Thomas S. Ashe.	11. John B. Baldwin.
6. Arch. H. Arrington.	12. Walter R. Staples.
7. Robert McLean.	13. Fayette McMullen.
8 William Lander.	14. Samuel A. Miller.
9. B. S. Gaither.	15. Robt. Johnston.
10. A. T. Davidson.	16. Charles W. Russell.

*SENATORIAL TERMS.

Alabama—Mr. Clay, 2 years; Mr. Jemison, 6 years.
Arkansas—Mr. Johnson, 2 years: Mr. Mitchell, 6 years.
Florida—Mr. Baker, 2 years; Mr. Maxwell, 4 years.
Georgia—Mr. Johnson, 2 years; Mr. Hill, 6 years.
Kentucky—Mr. Simms, 2 years; Mr Burnett, 6 years.
Louisiana—Mr. Semmes, 4 years; Mr. Sparrow, 6 years.
Mississippi—Mr. Phelan, 2 years: Mr. Brown, 4 years.
Missouri—Mr. Clarke, 2 years, Mr. Peyton, 4 years.

North Carolina—Mr. Davis. 2 years ; Mr. Dortsch, 4 years.
South Carolina—Mr. Barnwell, 4 years , Mr. Orr, 6 years.
Tennessee—Mr. Henry, 4 years. Mr. Haines, 6 years.
Texas—Mr. Wigfall, 4 years : Mr. Oldham, 6 years.
Virginia—Mr. Caperton, 4 years ; Mr Hunter, 6 years.
Those marked with the ‡ have been members of the United States Congress,

THE ARMY.

Generals—Cooper, Lee, Johnson, Beauregard and Bragg.
Lieutenant Generals—Longstreet, Polk, Hardee, Kirby Smith, Holmes, Pemberton, Ewell and A. P. Hill.
Major Generals—Rhodes, Pender, Bowen, Heath, Ransem, W. H. T. Walker, S. D. Loe, Cleburne, W. Smith, C. M. Wilcox.

THE NAVY.

Admiral—Franklin Buchanon.
Captains - L. Rosseau, French Forrest. J. Tatnall. V. M. Randolph, G. M. Hollins, D. W. Ingraham, S. Barrou, W. F. Lynch, J. L. Sterrett, R. Semmes, and — Brown.
Captains for the War—S. S. Lee and W. C. Whittle.

STATISTICS AND GLEANINGS FROM THE UNITED STATES CENSUS REPORT OF 1860.

OF SEXES.

The number of males in this country is greater than the number of females by about 730 000. In the newly settled States and Territories the excess of males is very great. The males of California outnumbered the females nearly 67,000, or about one-fifth of the population. In Illinois there are about 92,000 more males than females, or one twelfth of the entire number. In polygamous Utah the numbers are nearly equal. In Massachusetts females outnumber the males by nearly 57,000, and in New York by a small number

Thus, as we have described, in this vast country, inhabited by its busy millions of men and women, they must needs have done much in ten years of peaceful pursuits to enrich themselves, and the country of their birth or their adoption. Let us see what they have done, without noting near all their labors.

OF RAILROADS.

The magnificent system of railroads which now spreads like a net all over the States, from the Atlantic-ocean to the Missouri river, is essentially the work of the last decennium. Up to 1830, but one railway connected the great interior lakes with the tide water, and that was restricted in the carriage of freight except on the payment of canal tolls. Previous to the commencement of the last decade, by far the greater proportion of railways were in the Atlantic States—isolated lines for local traffic. There was then but one important line in the West— a rude construction, devoted to the carrying trade and manslaughter, between Cincinnati and Sandusky. What in 1830 was without form and void, so far as purposes of general internal commerce were concerned, is now reduced to shape and system, whereby seller and buyer, though half way across the continent apart, can trade like neighbors. By means of the vast, web of railways constructed during the decade, the international commerce of the country has grown into stupendous proportions. The tonnage per annum of the railways completed in 1860 is estimated at 26,000,000 tons, valued at $3,900,000,000. Three quarters of this huge internal commerce has been created since 1850. It is the child of American railway system—a trade among our own people, larger than that at stake when George III, in his endeavor to control the trade, lost both trade and people of his American colonies.

In 1850 there were 8 590 76 miles of railway in operation, whose construction had cost $196 660 148. In 1860 there were in operation, 30, 793, miles, costing $1,151,560, 829, the increase in mileage having been 22,204 miles, and in cost of construction, $853,900,681.

Of the thirty four states all had railways at the date of the census, except Minnesota and Kansas, Oregon had not quite four miles and California a little more than seventy. The New England States had 3,669, miles, costing $148,366,514 ; the Middle States, New York, New Jersey, Pennsylvania, Delaware and Maryland, 6,321. miles, costing $329,528,231 : the Southern Atlantic States, 5,454, miles, costing $141.739,629 ; the Gulf States, 2 250, costing $64 943,746. In Kentucky, 1 805 miles, costing $49,761,199 ; the Interior States, North, Ohio. Indiana, Michigan, Illinois, Wisconsin, Iowa, Missouri, 11.212 miles costing $413.541,410, and the Pacific States, miles, costing $3 680.000

In the free States the number of miles is 19,942, whose construction cost $827,031,497. In the slave States the number of miles is 10,634,27, the construction of which cost $324,529,332.

At the date of the census there were 403 miles of the city passenger railroads; which had been built at a cost of $14,862,840, in the cities of Boston, New York, Brooklyn, Hoboken, Philadelphia, Cincinnati and St. Louis The next census will doubtless show that the current decade will have been the era of progress in this class of improvements, There can hardly be less than 2000 miles of the city passenger railroads in the Union already.

OF MANUFACTURES.

The returns exhibit a very large increase of manufactures in all branches. The total value of domestic manufactures for the year 1850 was $1,019,106,616. Their value for the year 1860, as ascertained in part and carefully estimated for the remainder, is put down at $1.900,000,000 —an increase of more than 86 per cent in ten years. If to this amount were added the aggregate of mechanical productions below the annual value of $500—of which the census takes no account—the result, in Mr. Kennedy's words would be one of startling magnitude.

The number of manufacturing establishments whose annual productions exceed $500, is 129,300, of which there are 19.514 in the New England

States, 72,364 in the Middle States, 35,310 in the Western States, 13,026 in the Southern States, 4095 in the Pacific States and the Territories of Utah, Washington and New Mexico. The capital invested is $1,050,000,000, which is distributed among the different geographical divisions of the country as follows : New England $259,420,000 ; Middle States, $464,759,206 ; Western States, $196,909,475 ; Southern States, $100,665,000 ; Pacific States, $28,766,319. The value of the material used is set down at $1,012,000,000, and the annual product at $1,900,000,000 as before stated. The number of persons employed is 1,355,000, of whom 1,100,000 are males and 285,000 females.

Such are the footings up of figures as to manufactures. To speak of the subject in detail, would require more space than can here be spared. Suffice it, that they embrace in their productions all the mechanical contrivances which are needed by man—the mighty steam-engine with the power of a river, and the pin which hides itself in the rose of a lady's bonnet ; cables which hold fleets at safe anchor through the wildest storm, and silken thread which the breeze stirs ; the press which throws off thirty thousand papers in an hour, and the crotchet needle with which your adored companion was whilom mouth making your last lamp mat ; plows for the farmers, pens for the editors, guns and swords and ammunition for the soldiers ; stoves to cook with, beds to sleep on, clothes to wear ; —everything needful which the inventive genius of the world has discovered how to manufacture—can be, and is produced by the manufactures of America, which actually support, directly and indirectly, one-third of the population of this country—a number greater than all the people in the land when Jackson fought the battle of New Orleans.

The value of the nineteen leading manufactures for the year ending June 1st, 1860, are set down in round numbers, as follows : Flour and meal $224,000,000 ; cotton goods, $115,000,000 ; lumber, $96,000,000 ; boots and shoes, $90,000,000 ; leather, $72,000,000 ; clothing, $70,000,000 ; woolen goods ; $69,000,000 ; machinery, steam engines, etc, $47,000,000 ; printing, book job and newspaper, $44,000,000 ; sugar refining, $33,500,000 ; iron founding, $28,500,000 ; spirituous liquors, $25,000,000 ; cabinet furniture, $24,000,000 ; bar and other rolled iron, $22,000,000 ; pig iron, $19,500,000 ; malt liquors, $18,000,000 ; agriculture implements, $17,500,000 ; paper, $17,500,000 ; soap and candle , $17,000,000.

OF AGRICULTURE &c.

Population, resources, &c., of the Free and of the slaveholding States according to the census of 1860.

Population of the Free States..	18,907,753
Population of the slave States (Free)	8,039,789
Population of the slave States (Slaves)	3,950,511
Total population of the U. S., excluding the territories	31,151,046
The assessed value of real estate and personal property in the Free States was	$6,541,027,619
Ditto, in the Slave States	5,465,808,957
Total assessed value for the 34 States	$12,006,836,576
Average to each person in Free States was	$351
Average to each person in Slave States was	$650
The number of acres of improved lands in the Free States was	86,181,196
Ditto, in the Slave States	74,035,055
Total improved lands in the 34 States, acres	162,807,521
Number of improved acres to the person in Free States was	4 acres
In slave States was	9 acres
The cash value of farms, farming implements, and machinery in Free States was	£4,209,062,835
Ditto, in the Slaveholding States	2,676,476,321
Total value in United States of ditto	$6,884,539,156

Average value to the person in Free States was................ $233
In Slave States was................................ $372
The number of horses, asses and mules in the Free States was... ....   3 669,239
Ditto, to the slave States................................   3 527,236

Total number of horses, asses and mules in the United States.........   7,216,475

In Free States, five persons to each horse. In Slave States, two persons to each horse.]

SUMMARY OF MILCH COWS, WORKING OXEN, OTHER CATTLE, SHEEP AND SWINE.

In the Free States.		In the slaveholding States.	
Milch cows....	6 265 254	Milch cows.................	3,428,011
Working Oxen.............	1,011,868	Working Oxen....●..........	1,176,258
Other cattle,..........	6.412,206	Other cattle,..............	8.187,125
Sheep,...........~...........	15,357,312	Sheep,..................	7 064,116
Swine,.........~............	11,846,029	Swine,..................	20-651,182
	39,873,263		40,606,720
			39,873 268

Total number of milch cows, working oxen, other cattle, sheep and swine in the United States..................   80,879,988
In the Free States, two to each person. In the Slave States, five to each person..................................   ....
The value of live stock in the Free States was......................... $574,545,012
Ditto in the Slave States..................................   524,236,743

Total value of live stock in the 34 States $1,098,862,355
In the Free States average to each person. ....?......... $54
In Slave States,................................?..................   63
The number of bushels of wheat produced in the free State was......   120.170,315
Ditto in the slave States..................................   50 005,712

Total production of the 34 States, bushels....................   170,176.027
In free States each person has 6 bushels of wheat. In slave States each free person has 6 bushels, and each free and slave 4 bushels
The number of bushels of rye in the free States was........   16,897,079
And in the slaveholding states............................   4,067,677

Total production of rye in the 34 States, bushels,...................   20,965,046
The number of bushels of Indian corn produced in the free States was   392,756,464
And in the slaveholding States, ...   434,935.063

Total production of Indian corn in the 34 States, bushels............   827,694,528
In free States each person has 28 bushels of corn.   In slave States each free person has 51 bushels, and free and slave together have 35 bushels per head.
The number of bushels of oats produced in the Free States was   138,864,580
And in the slave States   33,224,515

Total production of oats in the 34 States, bushels.................   172,089,005
The total production of rice in the free States was, lbs....●.........   4,189
And in the slaveholding States, lbs... ....●.........   187,156 084

Total production of rice in the 34 States, lbs......................   187,140,173
The total production of tobacco in the free States was, lbs............   58,734,828
And in the slaveholding State, lb..........................   370 630,723

Total production of tobacco in the 34 States, lbs...................   429 364,751
The total production of ginned cotton in the free States was, bales of 400 lbs................................   6
And in the slaveholding States................................   5,196 938

Total production of ginned cotton in the 34 States, bales of 400lbs each   5,196,944
The total production of Irish and sweet potatoes, peas and beans in the Free States was—bushels.........................   103 494,758
And in the Slave States,................................   63 239,985

Total production in the 34 States of Irish and sweet potatoes, peas and
    beans—bushels, ... 166,724 735
The total production of wool in the Free States was—lbs., ... 45 247,012
And in the Slave States.. 14,695,316

Total production of wool in the 34 States—lbs 59,942,328
The total production of barley and buckwheat in the Free States was
    bushels,... 31,528,149
And in the Slave States—bushels................................... 1,656,546

Total production of barley and buckwheat in the 34 States—bushels 33,264,605
The value of orchard products and of the production of market gardens
    in the Free States was.... .... $25,804,014
And in the Slave States,... $9,103,216
Total value of orchard products and of the productions of market
    gardens in 34 States $34 907,230
The number of gallons of wine made in the Free States was.... 1,427,512
And in the Slave States.. 423,303

Total in the 34 States, gallons..................................... 1,550,519
The number of pounds of butter made in the Free States was........ 368,646 252
And in the Slave States... 91,026,870

Total production of butter made in the 34 States, lbs............... 459,672 053
The number of pounds of cheese made in the Free States was........ 104,531,006
And in the Slave States... 1,247,557

Total production in the 34 States lbs....... 105,782,052
The number of tons of hay made in the Free States was.............. 17,215,928

Total Sorghum molasses in the 34 States.............................. 7,176,042
The total production of maple molasses in the free States was, gallons 1,474,165
And in Slave States.. 470,144

The number of tons of hay made in the Free States was.............. 17,215,956
And in the Slave States.. 1,857,552

Total production of hay in the 34 States, tons...................... 19,073,506
The number of bushels of clover seed and grass seed made in the Free
    States was 1,508,060
And in the Slave States... 325,667

Total production of clover and grass seed in the 34 States, bushels.... 1,828,717
The number of tons of hemp, dew, water-rotted and otherwise pre-
    pared in the Free States was... 40,890
And in the Slave States... 63,590

Total hemp for the 34 States, tons.................................. 104 480
The total production of sugar cane made in the Free States, hhds of
    1,000lbs... 2-8
And in the Slave States... 301 972

Total production for the 34 States, hhds.............................. 302,806
The total production of cane molasses in the Free States was gallons 66
And in the Slave States.. 16,337 014

Total in the 34 States, gallons...................................... 16,337 050
Of Sorghum molasses, the free States made, gallons.................. 4,717,125
And in the slave States... 2,458,917

Production of the 34 States, gallons................................ 1,944 209
The production of maple sugar in the free States was, lbs............ 37,186,065
And of the slave States, lbs 1,677,523

Production of the 34 States, lbs.................................... 38,863,588
The production of hops in the free States was, lbs.................. 10,952,296
And in the slave States, lbs 37,537
Total production of the 34 States, lb............................... 11,647,823
The production of flax in the free States was, lbs.................. 2 945,680
And in the slave States, lbs... 1,733,9

Total flax in the 34 States, lbs.. 3,778,843
The product on of flax seed in the free States was, bushels............ 513,227
And in the slave States, bushels.. 98,553

Total production of flax seed in the 34 States, bushels............... 611,780
The production of silk cocoons in the Free States was, lbs.......... 5,370
And in the Slave States... 1,211

Total in the 34 States, lbs... 6,561
The product on of beeswax and honey in the Free States was, lbs..... 10,087,926
And in the Slave States.. 15,382,905

Total beeswax and honey for the 34 States, lbs...... 26,370,831
The value of home-made manufactures in the Free States.......... $5,699,727
And in the Slave States... 18,526,734

Total home made manufactures in the 34 States.................. $24,226,461
The value of animals slaughtered in the Free States............... $106,660,980
And in the Slave States.. 106,372,075

Total number of animals slaughtered in the 34 States........... $212,032,055

Theso tables when closely examined, will surprise even the most confident among us, as to our ability to maintain a long contest for our liberties. In all the necessaries of life we are greatly in excess of our enemies.

THE NEW TAX LAW.

1, The first section imposes a tax of eight per cent. upon the value of all naval stores, salt, wines and spiritous liquors, tobacco, manufactured or un-manufactured, cotton, wool, flour, sugar molasses, syrup rice and other agri-cultural products, held or owned on the first day of July 1863, and not nec-essary for family consumption for the unexpired portion of the year 1863, and of the growth or production of any year preceding the year 1863 ; and a tax of one per cent. upon all moneys, bank notes or other currency on hand or on deposit on the 1st of July 1863, and on the value of all credits on which the interest has not been paid, and not employed in a business, the income derived from which is taxed under the provisions of this act ; Provided, that all moneys owned, held or deposited beyond the limits of the Confederate States, shall be valued at the current rate of exchange in Confederate Treas-ury notes. The tax, to be assessed on the 1st day of July and collected on the 1st day of October 1863, or as soon thereafter as may be practicable.

2. Every person engaged, or intending to engage, in any business named in the 5th section, shall, within 60 days after the passage of the act, or at the time of beginning business, and on the 1st of January in each year thereafter, register with the district collector a true account of the name and residence of each person, firm or corporation engaged or interested in the business, with a statement of the time for which, and the place and manner in which the same is to be conducted, &c. At the time of the regis-try there shall be paid the specific tax for the year ending on the next 31st of December, and such other tax as may be due upon sales or receipts in such business.

3 Any person failing to make such registry and pay such tax, shall, in addition to all other taxes upon his business imposed by the act, pay double the amount of the specific tax on such business, and a like sum for every thirty days of such failure.

4. Requires a seperate registry and tax for each business mentioned in the 5th section, and for each place of conducting the same ; but no tax for mere storage of goods at a place other than the registered place of business. A

new registry required upon every change in the place of conducting a registered business, upon the death of any person conducting the same, or upon the transfer of the business to another, but no additional tax.

5 Imposes the following taxes for the year ending the 31st December, 1863 and for each year thereafter :

Bankers shall pay $500.

Auctioneers, Retail Dealers, Tobacconists, Pedlars, except persons pedling exclusively Books, periodicals and Newspapers, published in tae Confederacy, Apothecaries, Photographers and Confectioners, $30, and two and a half per centum on the gross amount of sales made. Mechanics and their Families who sell only the products of their labor, shall be exempt from Tax.

Wholesale dealers in liquors, $200, and five per centum on gross amount of sales. Retail dealers in liquors $100, and ten per centum on gross amount of sales.

Wholesale dealers in groceries, goods, wares, merchandise, &c., $200, and two and a half per centum.

Pawnbrokers, Money and exchange brokers, $200.

Distillers $200, and twenty per contum. Brewers $100, and two and a half per centum.

Hotels, Inns, Taverns, and Eating Houses, first class $500, second class $300, third class $200, fourth class $100, fifth class $50. Every house where food or refreshments are sold, and every boarding house where there shall be six boarders or more shall be deemed an eating house under this act.

Commercial brokers or commission merchants, $200, and two and a half per centum.

Theatres, $500 and five per centum on all receipts.

Each circus $100, and $10 for each exhibition. Jugglers and other persons exhibiting shows, $50.

Bowling alleys and Billiard rooms, $40 for each alley and table registered.

Livery Stable keepers, Lawyers, Physicians, Surgeons, and Dentists, $50.

Butchers and Bakers, $50, and one per centum. Catt'e Brokers $50, and two and a half per centum.

6. Every person registered is required to make returns of the gross amount of sales from the passage of the act to the 30th June, and every three months thereafter.

7. A tax upon all salaries, except of persons in the military or naval service, of one per cent. when not exceeding 1500, and two per cent. upon an excess over that amount. Provided, that no taxes shall be imposed by virture of this act on the salary of any person receiving a salary not exceeding $1 000 per annum; or at like rate for any other period of time, longer or shorter.

8. That the tax on annual incomes, between $500 and $1000, shall be five per cent. between $1,500 and $3 000, five per cent. on the first $1,500, and ten per cent on the excess between $3,000 and $5.000, ten per cent ; be tween $5,000 and $10,000, 12-1-4 per cent ; over $10,000, fifteen per cent.; subject to the following deductions ; on incomes derived from rents of real estate, manufacturing and mining establishments, etc., a sum sufficient for necessary annual repairs ; on incomes from any mining or manufacturing business, the rent, (if rented) cost of labor actually hired, and raw material ; on incomes from navigating enterprises, the hire of the vessel or allowance for wear and tear of the same, not exceeding ten per cent. ; on incomes derived from the sale of merchandize or any o her property, the prime cost, cost of transportation, salaries of clerks and rent of buildings ; on incomes from any other occupation, the salaries of clerks, rent, cost of labor, material &c., and in case of mutual insurance companies, the amount of losses paid by them during the year. Incomes derived from any other sources are subject to no deductions whatever.

All joint stock companies and corporations, shall pay one tenth of the dividened and reserved fund annually If the annual earnings shall give a profit of more than ten and less than twenty per cent. on capital stock, one eighth to be paid ; if more than twenty per cent. one-sixth. The tax to be collected on the first of January 1863 and of each year thereafter.

9. Relates to estimates and deductions, investigations, referees, &c.

10: A tax of ten per cent. on all profits in 1862, by the purchase and sale of flou·, corn, bacon, pork, oats, hay, rice, salt, iron, or the manufactures of iron, sugar, molasses made of cane, butter, woolon clothes, shoes; boots, blankets, and cotton cloths. Does not apply to regular retail business.

Tax in Kind

11. Each farmer, after reserving for his own use 50 bushels sweet, and 50 bushels Irish potatoes, 100 bushels corn or 50 bushels wheat, produced this year, shall pay and deliver to the Confederate Government one tenth of the grain, potatoes, forage, sugar, molasses, cotton, wool, and tobacco produced. · After reserving twenty bushels peas or beans, he shall deliver one-tenth thereof.

12. Every farmer, planter or graizer, one-tenth of the hogs slaughtered by him, in cured bacon, at the rate of 60 pounds of bacon to 100 pounds of pork ; one per cent. upon the value of all neat cattle, horses, mules, not used in cultivation, and asses, to be paid by the owners of the same, beeves sold, to be taxed as income.

13. Gives in detail the duties of post-quartermasters under this act.

14. Relates to the duties of assessors and collectors.

15. Makes trustees, guardians, &c., responsible for taxes due from estates, &c., under their control.

16. Exempts the income and moneys of hospitals, asylums, churches, schools, and colleges from taxation under the act.

17. Authori·es the Secretary of the Treasury to make all rules and regulations necessary to the operation of the act.

18. Provides that the act shall be in force for two years from the expiration of the present year, unless sooner repealed ; that the tax on naval stores. flour, wool, cotton, tobacco and other agricultural products of the growth of any year preceding 1863, imposed in the first section, shall be levied and collected only for the present year.

FINANCES OF THE CONFEDERATE STATES.

A condensed copy of that portion of the report of Hon. C. J. Memminger, Secretary of the Treasury, recently presented to Congress, which shows the fiscal operations of his department of the Government. and exhibits the amount and condition of the public debt on the 31st of December :

From the ommencement of the Permanent Government to the 31st December, 1862, the receipts and expenditures were as follows :

RECEIPTS.

Treasury notes, $215.554.885 ; interest-bearing notes, 113,740,000 ; call loan certificates, $59.742,796 ; one hundred millions loan, $41,398,286 ; war tax, $16,664,518 ; all other sources, $10,754,934. Total, $457,855,704.

EXPENDITURES.

War department, $541,011,754, navy department, $20,559,233 ; civil, miscellaneous, foreign interoourse and customs, $13,673,376 ; interest on public debts (loans) $5,892,989 ; payment of treasury notes;

Act March 9, 1861, principal $545,900— interest, $20,800—$566,761 ; redemption of six per cent. certificates, $11,516,400 ; redemption of treasury notes called in for cancellation and reimbursement of principal, under act of May 16, 1861, $23,751,170; total expenditures for "public debt," $41,727,322.

Balances against the Treasury on the 18th February, 1862, $23,437,579
Amount of Receipts $457,855,764
Deduct amount of expenditure........................... 443,411,397

Balance... $14,444,397

The balance consists in part of the coin on hand received from Bank of Louisiana, and the remainder in interest-bearing treasury notes

AMOUNT TO BE RAISED BY CONGRESS.

The appropriations made by Congress, and not yet drawn from the Treasury, amount to $81,879,913; estimates for the support of Government to 1st July, the end of the fiscal year, (including $249,977 for the War Department,) $290,493,713 Total $372,373,626. Deduct $14,444,397, balance in Treasury, leaving amount to be raised by Congress, $357,929,329.

THE PUBLIC DEBT.

The debt of the Government at the same date (December 21st, 1861) was as follows :

Bonds and Stock.

Under act February 28th, 1861,.............$14,987 000
Under act May 16th, 1861.................. 6,414,300
Under act August 19th, 1861..... 67,585,100
Deposit certificates under act December 21th, 1861 :
Issued....................$69,005,370
Redeemed.................. 12,516,400   56,158,970—145 475,370

Treasury Notes.

3.65 notes. 992,090
2 years notes............................. 10,919,025
General currency........... 272,022,467
7.30 notes................................ 127 480,000
$1 and $2 notes ....:........ 6,216,960— 419,629,692

$556,105,062

"In the above statement is a large amount of bonds and interest bearing notes which are on hand in the various depositories not yet issued. It is important to bear this in mind in estimating the effect of the act of the last session upon funding treasury notes. The loans in which such notes are funded are those mentioned in the schedule as loans of May 16th and August 19th. The amount of those loans as reported at the last meeting of Congress, was, on 1st of August, $41,577,250.
By the statement now reported, the total amount of these. -
bonds is..$73,999,400
From which should be deducted amount on hand not yet
disposed of, say..................... 8,000,000

$65,999,400

And in order to ascertain the amount of Treasury notes
funded, there must be deducted for the bonds issued for
produce, say... 7,000,000

                                                       $58,999,400
Deduct amount reported 1st August........................ 41,577,250

   Balance.. $17,422,150

This balance shows the amount of Treasury notes funded in five
months, the average being about three and a half millions per month.

INTEREST BEARING TREASURY NOTES.

During the same period, the interest-bearing Treasury notes have
increased from $22,799,900 to 120,480,000. Increase $97,680,100 ;
from which deduct notes on hand, $11,904,600. Real increase $85,-
775,500. This large increase of interest-bearing notes affords satisfactory evidence that the issue of them was a judicious increase, and for
any ordinary war, the bond and interest notes, amounting together to a
monthly sale of twenty and a half millions, would have sustained the
Government without any resort to paper currency. But the estimates
call for more than twice the amounts furnished by these resources, and
we are compelled to resort to Treasury notes to supply the deficiency."

The following Report has been compiled from the Statement of the
Register of the Treasury, issued August 18th, 1863 :

The whole amount of Treasury notes issued since the Government
went into operation is exactly $624,000,000. Of these there have been
funded in bonds and stocks $126,000,000, and about a million of notes
have been cancelled in connection with the postoffice and office of the
war tax. If we subtract the amount thus funded and cancelled from
the amount issued, there will remain outstanding $497,000,000 for pur-
poses of circulation and domestic exchange ; two hundred millions have
been invested in bonds and stocks, and to this sum must be added one
hundred and twenty-five millions in interest-bearing Treasury notes,
making a sum of three hundred and twenty-five million dollars of funded
debt.

The whole public debt, therefore, including the European loan, does
not quite reach the sum of eight hundred and forty millions, and against
this amount must be charged all the cotton and other assets of whatever
description, now held by the Government.

The entire interest of the public debt does not exceed twenty-three
million dollars—paid at the high rates of 8, 7.30 and 7 per cent.

—

* *Statement of Outstanding Treasury Notes, August 8, 1863.*

Total of all kinds of General Currency Notes.......................$382,114,406
Estimated on hand for cancellation.................................... 70,134,600

                                                 $452,979,806
And probable beyond the Mississippi. 180,000,000

                                                 $302,979,806

Statement of Bonds into which Currency has been Funded, including avails of the Produce Loan.

Total of 100 million loan...................................	$100 000,000
Funded since February 20th. 1863	1 4 31⁵ 370
Funded of notes; May 16th, 1861.........................	8,0⁶6 300
	$232 404 670
On hand, to be funded by estimate......................	70,000,000
Total funded.......................................	$302.404,670
Five per cent. call, partly funded.......................	15,442,000
Total..	$317,846,670

------◆◆◆------

THE RESOURCES OF THE CONFEDERATE STATES.

The census of 1860, taken by the authorities of the Government of the United States, as stated by John Schley of Augusta, Ga., in his pamphlet, represents the taxable property of the following eleven States, at $5,202,237,807, namely:

Virginia..............:..........	$7 3.219,681	Louisiana..................	$602,118 668
North Carolina	358,730 309	Texas	365 2 0 614
South Carolina..............	548. 38.754	Mississippi..................	6 7,324 911
Georgia	645.895.3 7	Arkansas..................	219 266 473
Florida................	73.112.5(0	Tennessee..................	483,963,8 2
Alabama................	495,237,678		

We allow a deduction from these figures of $1,202,237,807 and take the property at 4 000,000,000. and throw off all above that sum in 1860, and assume, as near the truth, that the same property, now put down at its market value in Confederate money will be all of $18,000,000 000.

Mr. Bullett an agent of Wm. H. Seward, sent by him from Washington to New O leans to report upon the cotton crop of the country, puts down the crop of 1861 at 4,000,000 bales, and puts down the amount in our hands at 3 500 000. Mr. Cridland, acting English Consul at Richmond, August 8th, 1862, puts down the quantity at 3,000,000 certainly on hand. Mr. R. Bunch, English Consul at Charleston, S. C., makes the quantity, August 13th, 1862, to be 3.950 000 bales. We extract these estimates from an official paper laid before the British Parliament upon the civil war in the United States, printed in 1863. The average value of a bale of cotton is now $175. Taking all on hand, the crop of 1861 and 1862, at 3,500,000. bales, we hold in this article about $600.000.000.

We estimate 100,000 hogsheads tobacco in the country, worth $50.000,000: in naval stores, pitch, tar. turpentine. and all other articles, as much more $50,000,000 —making in the aggregate, $700 000,-000—productions every day increasing in value, and which in fifteen months, has increased in value quite $500 000.000. In other words, our war expenditure for that period has been paid by the increased value of crops we held then and still have as a clear capital. Upon these crops 8 per cent. has been levied, and upon the incomes of the country about 12½ per cent. as the average—*besides licensed taxation*, which we throw in, as well as the tax on speculators in 1862. Our sum then is this, viz

The annual interest to pay on the public debt estimated by the Secretary
of the Treasury, on 1st July, 1863, at...... ....$48,000,000
The current Government expenses, other than those which are extraordinary (both of these items are over-estimated).................... 42,000,000

Say in all, interest, expense and outlays of all kinds................. $90,000,000
Tax on the crops and merchandise on hand.... ....,.......$56,000,000
Tax on incomes, being 6 per cent. on the taxable property—
$8,000,000,000—in round numbers......................:........48,000,000
                                                  ——104,000,000

    Surplus over all accounts..... ....$14,000,000

The tax in kind, or the one-tenth of all the crops, will yield the supplies for the army, except such goods as are of foreign growth. The
value of this item will be the one-hundredth part of the entire property.
viz : $80,000,000. We generally take the local interest as the net in-
come from all agricultural pursuits. The tax in kind is upon the gross
yield, and we place it at ten per cent. We may carry the principle of
taking the customs in kind into effect with profit and justice. The wis-
dom of taking taxes in kind is sanctified by the authority of Moses, and
our altered situation in a few months will be the best vindication of the
policy, which will dispense with the use of money to a very large extent.
We append the debts of the principal European nations, and their population, and the debt for each person in round numbers :

1857.	Gross Debt.	Popula'n.	Debt pr head.	Annual Revenue.
Great Britain and Ireland...........	$3,800,000,000	27,000,000	$140 00	$280,000,000
Austria.=	900,000,000	36,000,000	25 00	125,000,000
France.	1,375,000,000	35,000,000	40 00	310,000,000
Russia......:	870,000,000	54,000,000	16 00	175,000,000
Prussia....	160,000,000	17,000,000	9 00	75,000,000
Spain.............	600,000,000	14,000,000	43 00	75,000,000
Turkey.... ....,.....	40,000,000	11,000,000	4 00	32,500,000
Netherlands......................	500,000,000	4,000,000	125 00	30,000,000
Belgium......................	145,000,000	4,000,000	36 00	25,000,000
Denmark......................	67,750,000	2,000,000	34 00	7,500,000
Bavaria.....................	80,730,000	5,000,000	17 00	15,000,000
The two Sicilies....:.........	84,000,000	8,000,000	10 00	22,50 ,000
Sardinia...................	120,000,000	5,000,000	24 00	25,500,000
Hanover......................	27,370,000	2,000,000	14 00	6,500,000
Baden......	27,420,000	1,500,000	18 00	8,490,000
States of the Church............	100,000,000	3,000,000	34 00	11,965,000
Portugal....................	90,000,000	3,500,000	25 00	14,250,000
Kingdom of Saxony............	32,500,000	2,000,000	16 00	32,500,000
Sweden..........	——	3,500,000	——	5,200,000
Norway............	——	1,500,000	——	3,250,000
Tuscany......................	——	2,000,000	——	6,252,330
Greece....................	20,880,000	1,000,000	20 00	4,300,000
Modena................. ...	——	500,000	——	1,700,000
Parma..................	1,900,000	500,000	4 00	380,000
Wirtemburg....................	21,210,000	2,000,000	12 00	5,000,000
Smaller German States............	85,000,000	6,000,000	14 00	27,500,000
The Swiss Cantons................	——	8,000,000	——	3,250,000

We may double our present interest-bearing debt before we shall reach
the per capita debt of Great Britain ; but we have a landed property far
more valuable than any in the world; which alone will be worth as
much as all the property in Great Britain.—*Compiled from the Record*

VALUE OF THE LATE UNITED STATES.

The census of 1860 shows the following as the money value of the States :

States.	Assessed value of Real Estate.	Assessed Value of Personal Estate.	True value of Real and Personal Estate
Maine	$86 717.716	$67 662 672	$190.211 610
New Hampshire	59,638.346	64.171,743	156,310.860
Vermont	65 639.073	19,148.646	122 477,170
Massachusetts	475.4 3.165	301,744,651	815 237.443
Rhode Island	83.778 204	41.326,101	133.337,588
Connecticut	191,478 842	149,778,134	444.274 114
New York	1,069.654 080	820 816,558	1,843 338.517
New Jersey	151,161.742	143,520 550	467.918,324
Pennsylvania	581,192,9-0	158.060,355	1,416.501.818
Delaware	25,273,803	13 491 430	46,242 181
Maryland	65.341.438	231,793.800	376 949 914
Virginia	417.952.228	239 069,100	793 249 651
North Carolina	116,346 573	175,031.029	358,739 399
Florida	21,722.810	47.206,875	73,101 5 0
Alabama	155,134,089	277,164,673	495.237.078
Louisiana	280,704,-88	155.482.278	602 118.568
Arkansas	63,254.740	116,956.590	219,256 371
D. Columbia	83,197 542	7,087,403	41,064.845
Missouri	153,430,577	113.485.274	501,214 398
Kentucky	277 925.054	250,287 639	666 043.112
South Carolina	129 772,081	359 546 444	548,138 754
Illinois	287.219,940	101.987,432	871.860.262
Indiana	291,829 992	119.112,432	528,835,371
Texas	112 476,013	155.3 6.322	365 200.614
Kansas	16.088,602	6,429,630	31.327.895
Iowa	149,433,423	55 733,560	274,338,265
Tennessee	219 991,180	162,304 620	493 903 892
Michigan	123.605,084	39,927,921	257.143,983
Wisconsin	148.248,766	37,706,723	273.671,668
California	66.906,631	72,748 036	2 7,874,613
Minnesota	25,391,771	6.727,001	52.294,413
Ohio	687.518,121	272,348,9-0	1,193 848.422
Mississippi	157,836 737	351.036,175	607,324.911
Georgia	179.801.441	438,430,946	645.895.237
Oregon	6,279.602	12,745,313	28,930,637
New Mexico	7.018,260	13,828,529	20,813,768
Utah	586 501	3,861,616	5, 96,118
Washington	1,876.063	2,518.672	5,601.466
Nebraska	5,732,145	1,694,804	9,131,656

$16,159,916 086

THE SLAVE AND FREE STATES CONTRASTED.

Wherever, in the States, the people have enjoyed the advantage of slave labor, they have been distinguished by their general industrial prosperity and superiority in wealth and social happiness over similar communities, which have not enjoyed the use of slave labor.

Throughout all the slave holding States those counties which have had the greatest amount of slave labor have attained a higher degree of prosperity than any other counties in the United States, either North or South.

Throughout the slave labor, or more properly mixed labor States, those counties which approximate nearest to the condition of the white labor States by having the smallest number of negro slave laborers, are in the most backward condition, as to general prosperity and social progress, and contribute least to the support of government, education and religion.

As a matter of common observation by travelers and business men, it may be stated that of all social institutions which have ever been devised for improving the condition of society, and especially of the laboring population —for checking the progress of pauperism crime, and disease—for strengthening the spirit of constitutional liberty, and promoting the growth and diffusion of sincere religion, and of the spirit of friendship and brother-hood among men, negro slave labor has been the most efficient.

Throughout the mixed labor States the burthens of Government, education, etc., are chiefly supported by those counties which have a liberal supply of slave labor.

There is nothing speculative or uncertain in the vast aggregates of wealth produced by slave labor. It is an inexhaustible supply of wealth. The annual agricultural production of the mixed labor States forms a greater aggregate of value than the agricultural productions of the whole white labor States, with twice the population of white laborers. It may, therefore, be justly affirmed that agriculture in the mixed labor states is far more productive to the citizens, in proportion to the number, than the agriculture of the free labor States. Without running a complete parallel, we may glance at the following leading products, which indicate, as far as they go, that the people in the mixed labor States derive from agriculture twice as large returns, in proportion to their free population, as those of the free labor States, which had twice as many whites :

[1859-16 Mixed Labor States, including the District of Columbia.

Horses, Mules, Asses.	Cattle.	Hogs.	Bushel Corn and Wheat
1,769,065	9,784,850	20,507,313	376,968,267
	16 white labor States.		
2,298,058	8,484,793	9,596,068	313,776,136
	Excess in favor of mixed labor.		
270,207	1,253,057	11,301,545	68,192,181

This comparison could be rendered still more striking and satisfactory if time permitted the examination of all products, including cotton, tobacco, rice, and on the other hand, the manufacturing and mining products, in which the free labor States excel, but far less than is commonly supposed.

Mixed labor States are naturally more favorable to education and religion than exclusively free labor States. Free labor communities are always prevented by poverty from doing full justice to education by private action, and are never generally educated except by the authority of Government. * * * The excess of paupers in the free labor States in 1850 was 113,708, and their excess of convicted criminals was, in the sixteen free labor States, 19,459. When in the course of a few generations, the mixed labor States shall have scarcely one illiterate in five hundred, the free labor States will have a million of paupers and criminals, and in every reverse of trade a far greater number.

The assertion that slave labor is unfavorable to the spread of religion, is another of those reckless assertions which are believed, like the unprofitableness of slave labor and other falsehoods of the same group. The truth is that negro slavery has, in the United States, never hindered, but always favored religion, and has been the means of civilizing and of thoroughly Christianizing about twice as many of the heathen races as all the missionary enterprises of all Protestant Christendom combined. The negro race must either pass through the apprenticeship of slavery under the white race, to attain civilization or religion, or they must in time utterly perish, like other barbarians. In the mixed labor States, religion has been, perhaps, hindered in its propagation by the vastness of their territory and sparseness of their population. Nevertheless, they are not behind any other people in the evidences of piety. Under the delusive idea that African slavery was prejudicial to the welfare of the white race, the experiment of abolishing negro slavery was tried in the Northern States on a small scale -too small for the community to feel it as a calamity or to know its true result ex ept by careful investigation. We see one result in the fact that the most Northern States are the poorest, and pauperism is continually encroaching upon their laboring population, notwithstanding their laborious industry and pinching economy.

We see also that the emancipated negroes are a blighted race. They perish from poverty, vice and ignorance, and the loss of the friendly care of white families. From 1790 to 1850 they have increased. with all the additions by fugitives and by emancipation- probably 30,000 or 40,000—only from 67,479 to 196,026, while the slave negro population in the same time has increased from 657,257 to 3,204,313. Had the emancipation folly been embraced by all the States at the commence - ment of our national existence, and produced similar results in a l, the number of the negro population would have been in 1850 not 3,204,- 413, but 1,957,352. The emancipation law would have struck from existence 1,246,961 victims in the name of philanthropy, and the sur- vivors would have been, not the useful, orderly, and largely Christian l laborers that we now have, but would have been as free negroes are everywhere—an incumbrance upon society. The wealth of the nation would have been blighted to an extent of which Jamaica gives us an ex- ample, and instead of 465,000 professing Christians, religion would have declined among them, as it has among the blacks of the West Indies and New England, while from the ranks of these two millions of free negroes would have been supplied to our penitentiaries according to the statistics of negro criminality in New York in 1850, an army of 10,223 convicts, or, according to the statistics of Boston -the headquarters of ferocious philanthropy—they would have furnished for our "jails, houses of correction and refuge and alms-houses," one to every 1717, or in two millions an army of 123,685.

・   ――――――・●・――――――

THE STOCK OF COTTON IN THE CONFEDERATE STATES.

[From the Manchester Examiner.]

On this subject the following letter appears in a London cotemporary, from a Confederate source : In the several communications recently published concerning the stock of Cotton in the Confederate States, no allowance has been made for that consumed by the people of the South, who have depended, since the 1st of May, 1861, on their own manufactures for their dry goods   The quantity of their raw material thus taken up to the 1st of September next, will be equivalent to at least 1 500,000 bales, Cotton having been used for almost every conceivable purpose.   As nearly the whole crop of 1860 was exported, shipments continuing up to July, 1861, the following statement, based upon information from the Cotton States, may be regarded as a fair approximation to the number of bales at the commencement of the next commercial year :

		Bales.
Crop of 1861,		3,500.000
Crop of 1862,		1,000.000
Crop of 1863,		1,000,000
Total,		5,500,000
Exported,	150,000	
Destroyed,	850,000	
Consumed,	1,500,000	
		2,500,000
Stock on hand on the 1st September, 1863		3,000,000

Of this quantity, however, it is not likely that more than 2,000,000 bales could be sent to market prior to the close of the shipping season in 1864, under the most favorable circumstances, one half of which will be required by the manufacturers of the American States. Should peace be concluded by the first of July, more than a year thereafter would be needed to place the inland transportation facilities of the South in the same condition that they occupied previous to the war, and in the meanwhile the process of getting Cotton to the ports would not only be very tedious, but very expensive. The usual imports of Cotton into Great Britain consist of eighty per cent. American and twenty per cent. other sorts. The exports from here to the continent being principally of Surats, leave 85 per cent. American to make what are known as British fabrics, of which there was an extra large stock in all parts of the world at the breaking out of hostilities. In fact, the American crops of 1858, 1859 and 1860, averaged an excess of 1,000,000 each, or an accumulation in the three years of 3,000,000 bales beyond the wants of mankind.

●

This extra quantity received a fictitious consumption by being passed through fictitious looms, an additional spinning force of thirty per cent, having been put in motion when there was no occasion for such an increase as circumstances have proved. This was equal to a year's demand, which, with the ordinary two years' supply of Cotton and Cotton goods always on hand, made the importing countries independent of the South for the period of three years, assuming that the warehouses would be entirely emptied. Twenty-six months of that time have already elapsed, and thirty months will have transpired before any possible relief can be experienced. Cotton is now selling at Liverpool at "three prices," or famine rates. What, then, must be its value a few months hence? Surely the warehouse floors cannot be swept clean.

After two years of "agitation" on the subject, increased supplies do not come forward from India and other countries, the additional quantity thence not exceeding the great waste in the Federal States for the war purposes. Nor is it probable that there would be any demand for "outside" productions. They may answer for certain descriptions of manufactures for home use, but the great export trade of England is in goods made from American Cotton, and it seems folly to imagine that India can in any event occupy the place of America in this particular, unless by some freak of nature the peculiar climate influenced by the Gulf Stream, and other advantages possessed by the States for the culture of their staple, be transported to the far East. The average consumption on both sides of the Atlantic subsequent to the discovery of gold in California and Australia, has been about 3,000,000 bales per annum; for ten years preceding that epoch it was only 2,400,000 bales. It is reasonable to suppose then, that upon the recurrence of peace the demand will greatly increase.

On the 1st of September, 1863 there will be only one year's stock of raw Cotton at the old estimate, and the warehouses will contain but six months' supply of Cotton and Cotton goods; whereas they should have enough for two years. This makes a deficiency equivalent to 4,000 000 bales, taking into consideration the ordinary stocks, and 7,000,000 bales below what was in existence at the consuming points at the time of the fall of Fort Sumter. It will, therefore, require three or four seasons of excessive crops to bring Cotton down to its nominal price. Not only has the ordinary demand to be supplied, but the usual stocks have to accumulate. The capital withdrawn from the Cotton trade by reason of the American war has been the means of funding joint stock banks and financial associations; in turn, the same funds will pass through these new sieves into their accustomed channel.

The foregoing statement differs from one inserted in your columns some days ago to the extent of 1,500,000 bales, the writer of which overlooked the quantity consumed in the Southern States. This, however, does in no manner diminish the resources of the Confederacy; on the contrary, it augments the wealth of the people of the South, as 3,000 000 bales will net more money than 4,500,000 bales, the price ruling higher and expenses less. European as well as American statesmen, not being aware of the details of mercantile affairs, committed an error in thinking that the war would at once create a Cotton "pinch." They not only made no allowance for the usual two years' supply over in stock, but for the extra quantity, equal to an additional year's wants. Although the earth's productions that are used for food are rarely carried over the year of their growth, in consequence of their perishable nature, all those commodities required for clothing are generally held in sufficient quantities for two year's consumption.

THE CONFEDERATE FORCES.

We roughly estimate the number now in the field and rapidly forming for the field, as follows :

Confederate army, proper,	350,000
From conscription up to 45 years,	80,000
State levies under late call,	50,000
Volunteer exempts,	35,000
	515,000

The white males in the Confederate States, between 18 and 45 years, liable to conscription, exclusive of Maryland, Missouri, Kentucky and Delaware, is 1,115,000. Between the ages of 18 and 45, now called for there are in the remaining Southern States, over 900,000 men, exclusive of the Border States. Deducting 300,000 sick and disabled from this number, and we still have 600,000 men in and preparing for the field. The slaves of the South will supply us with food, if every man capable of bearing arms should be called to the field.

An estimate of the number of volunteer troops raised in some of the Confederate States previous to the enforcement of the conscript act :

Alabama,	65,000	South Carolina,	42,973
Georgia,	49,000	Maryland,	12,000
Florida,	17,000	Tennessee,	39,000
Mississippi,	71,000	Louisiana,	27,000
Texas,	48,000	North Carolina,	37,000
Virginia,	82,000		

THE NORTHERN ARMY.

A statement compiled from the United States Army Register, showing that the Regular Army of the United States consists of 2,388 commissioned officers and 40,626 men, making an aggregate of 43,074 men, and that the volunteer army consists of seventy regiments of cavalry, seventy of artillery, and eight hundred and sixty regiments of infantry, comprising 39,922 commissioned officers and 1,053,402 rank and file; being an aggregate of 1,092,402 of volunteers and a total of men in the field of 1,135,416.

A few figures, lately obtained from the Department of Agriculture, tell that our total agricultural exports, (exclusive of cotton) in 1860, when we were at peace, were $90,849,556 of which the Southern ports exported $19,738,365. In 1861, with half a million of men in arms, and no Southern exports, they amounted to $137,026,505, and in 1862, with a million of men in the field, (one half of them from the rural districts) and no Southern exports, they reached the sum of $155,142,075.

The amount of wheat and flour alone exported in the year ending September 1, 1862, exceeded that of the previous year by over seven millions of bushels. Estimating the force of our army (and its employers) in the field at one million of men, and it may be deemed a reasonable estimate, and the rations per diem to each man at twentytwo ounces of flour, it requires for its supply for a year 12,900 bushels of wheat.

---- •◆• ----

Population of some of the Principal Cities in the Southern States.

CITIES.	STATES	1850.	1860.
Baltimore	Maryland	169.054	212,418
New Orleans	Louisiana	116.375	172,786
St Louis	Missouri	77,860	160,479
Louisville	Kentucky	43,194	75,196
Charleston	South Carolina	37.889	48,494
Richmond	Virginia	21,570	39,860
Savannah	Georgia	15,312	23,739
Mobile	Alabama	20,515	24,720
Nashville	Tennessee	18,478	29,7-3
Memphis	Tennessee	10,841	29.830
Montgomery	Alabama	8,793	12,243
Augusta	Georgia	8,225	16,490
Natchez	Mississippi	4,439	7,321
Petersburg	Virginia	14,610	18,213
Norfolk	Virginia	14,336	18,966
Wilmington	North Carolina	7,263	12,362
Galveston	Texas	5,210	10,112
Vicksburg	Mississippi	4,740	7,420

---- •◆•• ----

OUR POSTAL SYSTEM.

The following figures show a very satisfactory exhibit of the present condition of our Postal Department :
The total receipts for the first six months of the present fiscal year. 1489.957 85
Total expenditures for the same period, . . . 1,447,317 29

Excess of receipts over expenditures, : . 42,640 65

This is a most gratifying result, compared with the heavy excess of expenditures of last year, and one that the country will contemplate with pleasure.

Rates of Postage.

Single letters not exceeding a half ounce in weight, to any part of the Confederate States, shall be each 10 cents.

An additional single rate for each additional half ounce or less.

Drop letters 2 cents each.

In the foregoing cases, the postage to be prepaid by stamps or stamped envelopes.

Advertised letters 2 cents each,

On Newspapers.

One cent shall be charged on each newspaper not exceeding three ounces in weight, and for every additional ounce, one half cent additional ; periodicals published oftener than semi-monthly shall be charged as newspapers; regular subscribers to newspapers shall pay their postage quarterly in advance, &c., &c.

On Periodicals.

Periodicals published oftener than semi-monthly shall be charged as newspapers.

Periodicals published monthly, not exceeding 2½ ounces in weight, 2½ cents per quarter, and for every additional ounce or fraction of an ounce, 2½ cents additional per quarter.

Semi-monthly, double that.

Bi-monthly or quarterly, 2 cents an ounce.

On Transient Printed Matter.

Every other newspaper, pamphlet, periodical and magazine, each circular not sealed, handbill and engraving, not exceeding five ounces in weight, 2 cents for any distance ; 2 cents additional for each additional ounce or less beyond the first three ounces.

In all cases the postage to be prepaid by stamps or stamped envelopes.

Franking Privilege.

The following persons only are entitled to the franking privilege, and in all cases strictly confined to official business :

Postmaster General.

His Chief Clerk.

Auditor of the Treasury for the Post Office Department.

Deputy Postmasters.

AN ACT to authorise the establishment of Express Mails.

The Congress of the Confederate States of America do enact, That the Postmaster General be and he is hereby authorised, if found practicable and necessary, to establish express mails for the conveyance of letters and government dispatches only, as a means of securing greater dispatch

than can be afforded by the regular mails ; and the lines of express mails
so established shall be deemed post routes.

Sec. 2. The rates of postage on such lines shall be fixed by the Postmaster General, but shall not exceed one dollar on a single letter not exceeding in weight one-half ounce, and at the same rate for any additional
half ounce or fraction of a half ounce, for any distance not exceeding five
hundred miles, and for any distance exceeding five hundred miles, double
the said rate to be so fixed. Provided, this law shall not repeal the laws
now in force regulating the ordinary mail service.

PRODUCTION OF BREADSTUFFS—STATISTICS FROM
THE CENSUS OF 1860.

The following statistics are derived from the last United States census
reports :

WHEAT, RYE AND CORN PRODUCED IN THE UNITED STATES IN 1860.

States.	Wheat. Bushels.	Rye. Bushels.	Corn. Bushels.
California	5,946,600	55,000	524,800
Connecticut	52,400	618,700	2,059,800
Delaware	913,000	27,250	3,892,400
Illinois	24,159,500	981,200	115,396,600
Indiana........................	15,219,100	400,200	69,631,600
Iowa...........................	8,433,200	176,060	41,117,000
Kansas........................	168,500	3,900	5,678,000
Kentucky.....................	7,394,800	1,055,300	64,043,400
Maine	233,900	23,300	1,546,000
Maryland	6,103,500	519,000	13,445,000
Massachusetts................	119,600	388,000	2,115,000
Michigan	8,313,200	494,200	12,552,100
Minnesota....................	2,195,800	124,300	2,685,600
Missouri	4,227,600	593,300	72,892,000
New Hampshire	239,000	123,300	1,414,700
New Jersey...................	1,763,100	1,439,500	9,723,300
New York.....................	8,681,100	4,787,000	20,961,000
Ohio..........................	14,532,000	656,100	70,637,100
Oregon	822,400	2,700	74,600
Pennsylvania.................	13,045,200	5,474,800	28,796,800
Rhode Island.................	1,100	26,300	459,000
Vermont......................	431,100	131,000	6,463,000
Wisconsin	15,812,600	887,500	7,565,300
Territories...................	1,007,400	11,200	2,767,200
Total bushels	139,816,500	18,803,100	549,786,700

Seceding States.	Wheat.	Rye.	Corn.
Alabama...................	1,222,500	74,000	32,761,200
Arkansas.................	955,800	77,900	17,758,700
Florida...................	2,800	21,300	2,834,500
Georgia..................	2,545,000	115,600	80,776,300
Louisiana.................	29,300	12,800	16,205,900
Mississippi...............	579,500	41,300	29,563,700
North Carolina............	4,743,700	235,800	80,078,600
South Carolina............	1,285,600	89,100	15,065,600
Tennessee................	5,409,000	260,300	50,748,300
Texas....................	1,464,300	95,000	16,521,600
Virginia..................	13,169,160	944,000	38,360,700
Seceding States..........	31,367,000	2,173,100	280,655,100
Other States.............	139,816,500	18,803,100	549,736,700
Totals, 1860.............	171,183,500	20,976,200	830,451,800
" 1850.............	100,476,000	14,188,800	592,071,000

The relative value of these products in the Federal and in the seceding States may be represented as follows:

	Wheat at $1.25.	Rye at 75c.	Corn at 50c.
Federal States..........	$174,770,000	$14,103,000	$274,893,000
Seceding States........	39,209,000	1,630,900	140,352,000
Total, 1860............	$213,979,000	$15,733,000	$415,225,000
" 1850..........	125,607,000	10,641,600	-296,025,000

From this official return it would appear that New York, which was in 1830–40, one of the leading wheat producing States, has now become the seventh, and is about on a parallel with Michigan in the article of wheat. Agriculturists state that the cultivation of wheat or any other article for a long series of years, without intermission, is an injury to the soil and to the crops. If New York would recover her position as a leading State in the production of wheat, more attention must be given to rotation of crops. The relative position of this State as a wheat producer, since 1840, is shown in the annexed summary of all the States producing over five million bushels each.

——— — — ·◆·— ·

THE RANGE OF PARROT GUNS.--In connection with the operations now in progress at Charleston it is interesting to know that a hollow shot weighing eighty pounds can be thrown from a 100 pound Parrot eight thousand four hundred and fifty-three yards, with a charge of No. 7 powder. With a charge of No. 5 powder the same shot can be thrown eight thousand eight hundred and forty-five yards. This is forty-five-yards over five miles. By increasing the charge of powder the range can be considerably augmented. The elevation of the gun to attain this great range is so considerable as to materially reduce the number of firings the gun will bear

POPULATION OF THE UNITED STATES.

ABSTRACT FROM THE CENSUS OF 1861.

STATES.	Whites.	Slaves.	Total.	White Males betw'n 18 & 45
Alabama	529,164	435,132	964,296	106,000
Arkansas	324,324	111,104	435,427	65,000
California	380,015		380,015	76,000
Connecticut	460,151		460,151	92,000
Delaware	110,420	1,798	112,218	22,000
Florida	78,686	61,753	140,439	16,000
Georg a	595,097	462,230	1,057,327	119,000
Illinois	1,711,753		1,711,753	342,000
Indinna	1,350,479		1,350,479	270,000
Iowa	674,948		674,948	135,000
Kansas	107,110		107,110	21,000
Kentucky	930,223	225,490	1,155,713	186,000
Louisiana	376,913	332,523	709,433	75,000
Maine	628,276		628,276	126,000
Maryland	599,846	87,188	687,034	120,000
Massachusetts	1,231,065		1,231,065	246,000
Mississippi	354,499	436,696	791,395	71,000
Missouri	1,058,352	114,555	1,173,317	211,000
Michigan	749,112		749,112	150,000
Minnesota	162,022		162,022	32,000
New Hampshire	326,972		326,972	65,000
New Jersey	672,031		672,031	134,000
New York	3,887,542		3,887,542	778,000
North Carolina	661,586	331,081	992,667	132,000
Ohio	2,339,599		2,339,599	468,000
Oregon	52,464		52,464	10,000
Pennsylvania	2,906,370		2,906,370	581,000
Rhode Island	174,621		174,621	35,000
South Carolina	301,271	402,541	703,812	66,000
Tennessee	834,063	275,784	1,109,847	167,000
Texas	420,651	180,388	601,039	84,000
Vermont	315,116		315,116	63,000
Virginia	1,105,196	490,887	1,596,083	221,000
Wiscousin	775,873		775,873	155,000
TERRITORIES.				
Colorado	34,197		34,197	6,000
Dakotah	4,839		4,839	1,000
Nebraska	2-,832	10	28,842	6,000
Nevada	6,587		6,587	1,000
New Mexico	93,517	24	93,541	13,000
Utah	40,266	29	40,295	8,000
Washington	11,578		11,578	2,000
District of Columbia	71,895	3,181	75,076	14,000
Total Population	27,477,090	3,962,801	31,429,891	5,484,000

THE PUBLIC DEBT OF THE NORTH—OFFICIAL STATEMENT.

The following is put forth as a full statement of the public debt of the North, July 1, 1863 :

Interest Bearing Debt.

4 per cent. temporary loan (coin) ·	$ 5,036,037 30	
4 per cent. temporary loan . . .	23,023,258 19	—$ 28,059,295 49
5 per cent. temporary loan . . .	70,808,187 91	
5 per cent. temporary loan (coin) .	6,450 00	
5 per cent. bonds, due 1865 .	3.461,000 00	
5 per cent. bonds, due 1871 . .	7,022,000 00	
5 per cent. bonds, due 1874 . .	20,000,000 00 —	101,297,538 91
6 per cent bonds, due 1868 , .	18,323,591 89	
6 per cent. bonds due 1881 . . .	69,517,800 00	
6 per cent. bonds, due 1882 ; .	185,684,141 26	
6 per cent. Treasury notes . .	717,100 00	
6 per cent. certificates of indebtedness	157,093,241 65 ·	431,275,874 71
7.30 per cent. bonds, due August 10, 1864 . . ·. ˙	52,931,000 00	
7.30 per cent. bonds, due October 1, 1864 . . . ·	86,989,500 00 —	139,920,500 00

Debt not bearing Interest.

Treasury Notes past due . .	$ ·32,100 00	
U. S. Notes . $357,646,589 60		
less amount in Treasury . 11,157,088 12—	376,439,500 88	
Fractional Currency , ,	20,192,456 00—	$ 396,721,056 88
Total debt, July 1, 1863, as exhibited by the books of the Treasury Department . . !		$1,097,274,365 99
Total debt, July 1, 1863, as estimated by the Secretary in report of December, 1862 . .		1,122,297,403 24

Actual debt less than the estimated debt   . $25,023,037 25

Recapitulation.

Aggregate debt at 4 per cent. interest . . .	$28,059,295 49	
Aggregate debt at 5 per cent. interest . ·. .	101,297,638 91	
Aggregate debt at 6 per cent. interest . . . ·	431,275,874 71	
Aggregate debt at 7.30 per cent. interest . . .	139,920,500.00	
Aggregate debt without interest	376,731,056 88	
Total debt, July 1, 1863, as exhibited by the books of the Treasury Department . . .	$1,097,274,365 99	

POPULATION OF THE CONFEDERATE STATES,
ACCORDING TO THE CENSUS OF 1860.

STATES.	White.	Slaves.	Total.
Virginia	1,097,373	495 826	1,593,100
North Carolina	697 965	328 377	1,008,342
South Carolina	308.186	407,185	715.371
Georgia	615 336	467.461	1,082.797
Florida	81,865	93,809	145,604
Alabama	520,444	435,473	935,917
Mississippi	407,551	497,607	887,158
Louisiana	354,245	312,186	666,431
Arkansas	331.710	109,065	440,775
Texas	515,999	184,956	600,955
Tennessee	859,528	287,112	1,146,040
Missouri	1,185,590	115,619	1,145,567
Kentucky	920,077	225,490	1,301,209
	7,895,869	3,960,166	11,669,956

POPULATION OF THE TERRITORIES.

Territories.	Population in 1850.	Population in 1860.
New Mexico,	61,547	93,024
Arizona,		9.600

RAILROADS IN THE CONFEDERATE STATES.

STATES.	Total length of lines—Miles.	Miles in Operation.	Act'al len'h in statute miles.	Cost Roads and Equipments.
Alabama,	1822	798	628	$20,975.639
Arkansas,	791	38	35	1,130,110
Florida.	730	289	279	6,308.699
Georgia,	1617	1241	123	25,087,220
Kentucky,	698	458	510	13,882,062
Louisiana,	1160	419	295	16,073,270
Mississippi,	545	365	691	9,024,444
Missouri,	1357	723	725	31,771,116
North Carolina,	1620	770	703	13,638,450
South Carolina,	1136	807	900	19,083,343
Tennessee,	1434	1062	977	27,358,141
Texas,	2667	284	385	7 578,943
Virginia,	2058	1525	1752	43,069,360
Total	16825	8779	9026	$235,660,816

CIRCUIT COURTS OF THE CONFEDERATE STATES.

PLACES AND TIMES OF HOLDING.

Alabama, Mobile, 2d Monday in April and 4th Monday in December.

Arkansas, Little Rock, 2d Monday in April.

Georgia, North District, Marietta, 2d Monday in March and September.

Georgia, South District, Savannah, 2d Monday in April—Milledgeville, Thursday after 1st Monday in November.

Kentucky, Frankfort, 3d Monday in May and October.

Louisiana, New Orleans, 4th Monday in April and 1st Monday in November.

Mississippi, Jackson, 1st Monday in May and November.

Missouri, St. Louis, 1st Monday in April and (special) October.

North Carolina, Raleigh, first Monday in June and last Monday in November.

South Carolina, Charleston, first Monday in April—Columbia, 4th Monday in November.

Tennessee, middle district, Nashville, 3d Monday in April and October.

Tennessee, east district, Knoxville, 3d Monday in May and 4th Monday in November.

Tennessee, west district, Jackson, first Monday in April and October.

Virginia, east district, Richmond, first Monday in May and fourth Monday in November.

Virginia, west district, Lewisburg, first Monday in August.

DISTRICT COURTS.

PLACES AND TIMES OF HOLDING.

Alabama, north district, Huntsville, second Monday in May and November.

Alabama, middle district, Montgomery, fourth Monday in May and November.

Alabama, south district, Mobile, fourth Monday in April and second Monday after 4th Monday in November.

Arkansas, east district, Little Rock, first Monday in April and October.

Arkansas, west district, second-Monday in May and Nov.

Florida, north district, Tallahassee, 1st Monday in January, Apalachicola, first Monday in February; Pensacola, first Monday in March; St. Augustine, first Monday in April.

Florida, south district, Key West, first Monday in May and November.

Georgia, north district, Marietta, second Monday in March and September.

Georgia, south district, Savannah, second Tuesday in February, May, August and November.

Kentucky, Frankfort, third Monday in May and October.

Louisiana, east district, New Orleans, third Monday in February, May and November.

Louisiana, west district, Opelousas, 1st Monday in August; Alexandria, first Monday in September; Shreveport, 1st Monday in October; Monroe, 1st Monday in November; St. Joseph, 1st Monday in December.

Mississippi, north district, Pontotoc, first Monday in June and December.

Mississippi, south district, Jackson, fourth o nday in January and June.

Missouri, east district, St. Louis, third Monday in February, May and November.

Missouri, west district, Jefferson City, first Monday in March and September.

North Carolina, Edenton, third Monday in April and Oct; Newbern, fourth Monday in April and October; Wilmington, first Monday after 4th Monday in April and October.

South Carolina, east district, Charleston, 1st Monday in January, May, July and October.

South Carolina, west district, Greenville court house, first Monday in August.

Tennessee, east district, Knoxville, third Monday in May and 4th Monday in November.

Tennessee, middle district, Nashville, third Monday in April and October.

Texas, east district, Galveston, 1st Monday in May and December; Brownsville, 1st Monday in March and October.

Texas, west district, Austin, 1st Monday in January and June; Tyler, fourth Monday in April and first Monday in November.

Virginia, east district, Richmond, 12th May and 12th November; Norfolk, 30th May and 1st November.

Virginia, west district, Staunton, 1st May and 1st October;

Wythe court house, 4th Monday in May and October; Charleston, 19th April and 19th September; Clarksburg, 24th March and 24th August; Wheeling, 6th April and 6th September.

WORTH KNOWING.—The first piece of artillery we know of was made by Schwartz, a German cordelier, soon after the invention of gunpowder, in 1330 Artillery is said to have been used by the Moors at Algesiras, in Spa'n. during the siege of 1341. Our historians say Edward III. had four pieces of cannon at Cressey, in 1346, which gained him the battle. The Venetians first used cannon at sea in 1377 against the Genoese. First used by the English in 1383. Bombs are said to have been invented at Venlo, a town of the Netherlands. in 1495, but did not come into general use until 1634, having been previously used only in the Dutch and Spanish armies. Mortars for throwing bombs were first made in England in 1543. The colossal mortar of Robert Mallet threw a shell weighing two thousand five hundred and fifty pounds, one mile and a half horizontally, with a charge of seventy pounds of powder. Bomb-vessels were first used at Algiers, in 1816, by a French engineer named Renau. Infernal machines were first used at Antwerp, in 1583. The French were first taught the art of throwing shells at Mothe, during the siege of 1634, by an English engineer. The first experiment of firing artillery *a richochet*, was made at Philipsburg, a town of Baden, in 1734.   Artillery was first used in sieges at Romorentin, in France, in 1256. The experiment to reduce a fortress by springing globes of compression was made at Schweidnitz, in Prussian Saxony, about 1762. The method of throwing red hot balls with certainty, was first prac'iced at Stralsund, in Prussia, when besieged by Wallenstein, about 1675.

Some of the Principal Colleges and Professional Schools in the Confederacy.

NAME	PLACE	Vols. in Lib'y.	Commencement of Session.
Southern University	Greensboro, Ala.	21 000	First Thursday in June.
University of North Carolina	Chapel Hill, N. C.	18 250	First Wednesday in August
Franklin	Athens, Ga.	24 000	First Monday in December
South Carolina	Columbia, S. C.	12 000	First Thursday in July.
University of Alabama	Tuscaloosa, Ala.	6 300	Last Thursday in July.
University of Louisiana	New Orleans, La.		July.
Centenary College	Jackson, La.	3 75	Last Thursday in July.
Mississippi College	Clinton, Miss.	3 000	Last Thursday in June.
Howard	Marion, Ala.	8 700	Fourth Wednesday in Aug.
Mercer University	Penfield, Ga.	18 250	First Wednesday in Aug.
Oglethorpe	Milledgeville, Ga.	21 000	First Thursday in June.
Davidson	Mecklenburg, N. C.	3 600	June 29th.
University of Virginia	Charlottesville, Va.	8 000	Fourth Thursday in June.
Randolph Macon	Boydton, Va.	9 866	Last Thursday in June.
University of Nashville	Nashville, Tenn.	650	Not in session at present.
University of Mississippi	Oxford, Miss.		Last Thursday in July.
Semple Broaddus	Cintao Hill, Miss.		Constantly in session.
Dorbear's Commercial	New Orleans, La.		
East Tennessee	Knoxville, Tenn.	8 000	First Wednesday in July.
Transylvania	Lexington, Ky.	14000	Last Thursday in June.
Union	Murfreesboro, Tenn.	4 300	First Wednesday in July.
Medical College of Alabama	Mobile.		
St. Louis	St. Louis, Mo.		
Wofford College	Spartanburg, S. C.	22,69.	

RANGE OF THE HUMAN VOICE.—The range of the human voice is quite astounding—there being about nine perfect tones, but 17,592,-186,044,515 different sounds; thus, 14 direct muscles, alone or together, produce 16,386; 30 indirect muscles, ditto, 173,741,823—and all in co operation, produce the number we have named; and these independently of different degrees of intensity. A man's voice ranges from bass to tenor, the medium being what is called a baritone. The female voice ranges from contralto to soprano—whereas, a boy's voice is alto, or between a tenor and a treble.

THE ARMIES OF EUROPE.

In the course of the season just concluded, a lecture on "The Armed Forces of Europe," was delivered at the United Service Institution, by Capt. 'Petrie, of Her Majesty's 14th regiment, employed on the topographical staff. The subject is one so full of interest, and so constantly discussed, that we willingly avail ourselves of Capt. Petrie's great carefulness and research for the means of supplying our readers with the information which they would otherwise find it difficult to obtain at all, or, if it were obtained, it would fail to possess such a character of authenticity as obviously distinguished the statements which we now reproduce :   -

AUSTRIA.—The war establishment of the Austrian army, according to the organization that came into force in April, 1860, is as follows : Three hundred and nine battalions of infantry, 487,954 ; forty-one regiments of cavalry. 60,110 ; one hundred and thirty-six battalions of artillery, 27,176 , guns, 1 098 ; regiments of engineers, 7 480 ; six regiments of pioneers, 6.850 twenty-four squadrons trains. 18 204 ; ten companies of sautary corps 2,550 ; staff corps, corps of adjutants and general staff, 3,389 ; total regular army, 563,211 ; volunteer corps organized in 1859. 35,000 ; depots and reserves of all arms, 103,751 ; gendarmerier police and veterans, etc., 42,382 ; grand total of forces, 738,344 ; total guns, 1 088.

PRUSSIA.—Infantry—Guard. nine regiments, 28,674 ; line seventy-two regiments. 229 392 ; jager, ten batalions. 10.460 ; total, 268,546. Cavalry—forty-eight regiments, 36.766 ; field jager and staff orderlies, 902 ; total, 37,670 Artillery—nine regiments. 41,292 ; guns, 1.228 Pioneers, tra'n, etc., 11.971' total field troops ; 359,479. Depots and Ersatz troops, 98,437 ; guns, 210. Landwehr and garrison troops, etc ; 261,126; grand total of forces. 719,092 ; total guns. 1,444

RUSSIA.—The army of Russia is so complicated in its organization that there would be considerable difficulty in making an analysis of it, but the numbers have been ascertained with sufficient accuracy to be on the present reduced establishment about 850,000 men. Of these the active army numbers 520 523 men, and 1.160 guns ; the rest are composed of disciplined Cossacks and irregular troops,

FRANCE—The infantry consists of one hundred and two regiments of the line, each having three active battalions and one depot battalion, twenty battalions of Chasseurs, three regiments of Zouaves. two regiments of foreign infantry, two battalions of African Light infantry, and three regiments of Turcos, or Tirailleurs Algerina. The artillery includes four regiments of horse artillery. with one hundred and ninety-two guns, ten regiments of mounted artillery, with six hundred guns, ten batteries of foot, with sixty guns. one regiment of pontooners, six squadrons train ; giving a total of 38.767 men, 37.960 horses. and 852 guns. This, in addition to 15.000 men. garrison artillery, and the depots' artificers, etc. The total number of guns that can be brought into the field, including the Imperial Guard, is 942, all of which are of brass and rifled.

The Imperial Gua d forms a complete co 'ps d'armee in itself. It is composed as follows : One regiment of gendarmerie, one regiment of grenadiers and voltigeurs. one regiment of chasseurs, one squadron of gendarmerie-a-cheval, six regiments of cavalry, fifteen batteries of artillery, two companies of pontooners, two companies of engineers. four companies of train. Its total establishment is 38.099 men. 13,447 horses. and 90 guns. The official returns, on the first of January. 1860, gave the total number of available men as follows : Troops in France, 398.559 ; in Algeria..83,782 ; North Italy, 55 281 : 7.901 : China, 5,468—total under arms 550,994 ; men on congo, 64,471 ; reserve, 11 017 grand total, 626.482.

GREAT BRITAIN.—Regular troops of all arms. 218.971 ; horses, 30,072 ; guns, 366 ; British local and colonial troops, 18,249 ; guns, 248 ; foreign and colored troops. chiefly in Indiana, 218,013 ; guns, 58, military police in India, 79,264 ; grand total, 534,527 ; horses, 30,072 ; guns, 672, Of these there are in the United Kingdom s Infantry—Guards, seven battalions, 6297 ; lide, thirty-five battalions, 33,105 ; total 39, 302. Cavalry—Life and horse guards, three regiments, 1311 ; dragoons, etc., sixteen regiments, 10,560 ; total, 11,874. Artillery—Horse, six batteries, 1299 ; guns, 36 ; field, 23 batteries. 5060 ; guns. 138 ; garrison. thirty-nine batteries. 4,680 ; 10,940 ; guns, 174 ; engineers, 2,816 ; military train, 1,830 ; hospital corps, 609 ; commissariat staff corps, 300 ; grand total of active force, 67,269 ; guns, 174. Besides there are the depot establishment ; Infantry—line, 120 depots, 24-779 ; cavalry. 9 depots, 396 ; artillery, 2.675 ; total depots, 24,141. Reserves available for the defense of the kingdom in case of war ; Pensioners, 14,789 militia. 45.000 : yeomanry. 16 000 ; Irish constabulary. 12,393 ; volunteers, 240,000 ; total, 329,276.

THE ATLANTIC TELEGRAPH.—The Atlantic telegraph project—now in the full tide of prosperity —seems destined to an early realization. The circular and prospectus of the company, under the sanction of Cyrus W. Field. of New York. It is estimated that the profits of business to be transacted through the cable will enable the company to pay eighteen per cent. interest to stockholders, and also to lay eight additional cables within the next seven years, without calling for more capital. The line would thus consist, in 1870, of nine cables. each of which will do its separate work. When this extensive machinery is in operation, the amount of business done must be immense, and the profits proportional. It is stated that the California overland telegraph has already paid for itself. If this is true, the pecuniary prospects of the Atlantic telegraph are brilliant.

The chances for profit of course rest upon the question of feasibility. There are data. however, which seem to settle the question, so far as it can be settled beforehand. Messrs. Glass, Elliott & Co., of London. the great manufacturers of submarine cable, submit a statement of the various cables laid by them, which amount in the aggregate to three thousand nine hundred and twenty-nine miles, all of which is now in working order, except a short line on the English coast. which was taken up on account of the interference of ships' anchors. One of their cables, connecting Malta and Alexandrin, is one thousand five hundred and thirty-five miles long, or nearly as long as the Atlantic cable. It has been working a year, in the most satisfactory manner. Some of their cables lie in fifteen hundred fathoms, or a mile and three-quarters depth of water.

The history of submarine telegraphing is contained in the brief and unpretentious record of Messrs Glass. Elliott & Co. They commenced eight years ago to lay telegraphic cables, and within that time have spanned the inland seas of Europe with no less than thirty cables. They connect England with France, Holland, Denmark and the Isle of Man ; France with Algiers, Italy with Corsica and Sardinia ; Egypt with Spain ; India with Ceylon ; Sweden with Denmark ; besides many points of lesser note, which complete a network of communication that. bids defiance to all the obstacles of space. They are now connecting England with India by a series of submarine cables and overland telegraph lines, which will reach nearly half around the world. Nearly four thousand miles of their submarine telegraph is now operating in the bottom of the sea, and if their assertion may be believed, no cable laid outside of anchorage ground has ever cost a shilling for repairs. With these results accomplished in so short a space of time, what may we not expect in the future ?

HORSES AND CATTLE IN THE WORLD.—An illustrated natural history of the animal kingdom has just been published by S. G. Goodrich.— Among other information abounding in it, it contains the following which is an estimate of the number of horses in various parts of the world. From this we extract the following :

The general estimate has been 8 to 18 horses in Europe to every hundred inhabitants. Denmark has 45 horses for every hundred inhabitants, which is more than any other European country.

Great Britain and Ireland have 2,500,000 horses.

France has 3,000,000

Austrian Empire, exclusive of Italy, 2,500,000.

Russia has 3,500,000.

The United States have 5,000,000 horses, which is more than any European country ; the horses of the whole world are estimated at 57,420,000.

Russia 20,000,000 cattle

Great Britain and Holland have 8,000,000.

Austria has 19,000,000.

France has 8,000,000.

United States of America have 22,000,000.

The world is estimated to contain 210,000,000. It is supposed that one-third of them are killed annually, so that we have about 23,000,600 bodies, 70,000,000 skins, 140,000,000 horns, 280,000,000 feet annually —to be converted into beef tallow, leather, combs, manure, etc.

DIARY OF THE WAR

AND CHRONOLOGY OF THE REMARKABLE EVENTS OF
THE PRESENT REVOLUTION.

(Continued from the Confederate States Almanac for 1863.)

1862.

November 19. A large force of Yankees landed at St. Mary's, Ga.; they were repulsed and driven back to their boats, when they commenced a furious bombardment on the city, doing great damage. Federal loss 8 killed.

November 19. Demonstration of the enemy at Lavergne. Gunboat attack of the enemy upon Fort McAllister, Genesis Point, Ogeechee river.

November 20. Colonel Howard, of the Alabama Cavalry, captured a drove of 5,000 hogs, and gained other advantages near Burkesville, Ky.

November 21 Surrender of Fredericksburg demanded by the Yankees and refused by Gen. Lee. Panic flight of Seigel's corps from Manassas, caused by nine scouts, who destroyed the stores left by him.

November 23. Confederate pickets captured near Barhamsville, Va. Mutiny of a Yankee regiment at Corinth.

November 25. Cavalry demonstration on the Confederate pickets at Suwanee, above Suffolk, Va Major Cox's Tennessee Cavalry destroyed Henderson station, on the Mobile and Ohio Railroad.

November 26. An Iron Yankee steamer destroyed in New River, N. C. Incursion of Confederate cavalry upon Maryland; two telegraph operators captured at Poolesville.

November 27. Skirmish at Lavergne, in which 100 of the 1st and 15th Alabama regiments sustained the attack of five regiments of infantry with artillery; the place was re occupied by the Confederates. A Yankee gunboat destroyed in Craven county, N. C. The steamboat Lone Star, with a crew of twenty-three men, captured below Plaquemines by a party of Terrell's Cavalry and volunteers, six in all.

November 28. Hampton's Cavalry captured 90 prisoners in Sufiolk county, Va

November 30 Yankee gunboats repulsed on Yazoo river by Wither's artillery. An earthquake felt-at Cairo and St. Louis.

' November 28, 29. Skirmishing at Holly Springs, Miss. Confederates forced to retreat, with a loss of 5 killed. Enemy's loss, 18 killed.

November 29—Dec. 1 Fighting near Abbeville, Miss. The Confederates compelled to fall back before an overwhelming force of the enemy. Considerable loss on both sides. The Confederates fall back beyond the Tallahatchie River.

December 1st. Great bombardment at Galveston, Texas. Several citizens killed and wounded.

December 1st. Fight at Snickersville Gap, Va. The Abolitionists routed after a severe contest, and 9 killed. Confederate loss 7 killed and 18 taken prisoners.

December 2. A party of Confederate cavalry made a dash into a Yankee camp in Westmoreland county, Va., and captured 48 prisoners and destroyed their camps and stores.

The Democrats carried the late election in New York by 12,000 majority. Republicanism rebuked.

December 3. The Yankees entered Winchester, Va., and retired before the Confederate forces sent to give them battle.

December 3. Fight at mouth of San Bernard River, Texas. A large force of Abolitionists were surprised and routed with considerable loss on the part of the enemy. Skirmish at Bird's Mill, Tenn. Forty-eight Yankees captured on the Rappahannock.

December 3, 4. Skirmishing near Oxford, Miss. Abolitionists repulsed in several brisk engagements. Confederate loss, 8 killed.

December 4. Bombardment of Port Royal, Va. The enemy repulsed and their gunboats damaged by our batteries. Attack on St. Marks, Fla. The enemy repulsed.

December 3, 4. Fighting at Water Valley, Miss. Confederates defeated with considerable loss. A large amount of confederate stores and money captured by the enemy Federal loss 20 killed and wounded.

December 4. Skirmish near Tuscumbia, Ala. Confederates taken by surprise and 70 captured as prisoners. Federal loss 9 killed and 22 wounded.

December 4. Skirmish on Rappahannock below Port Royal. Yankees routed and 50 captured.

December 5, C. Battle of ———, Miss. A desperate fight took place, in which the abolition army were completely defeated and chased in their ingoing of Mississippi. Confederate loss 10 killed and 40 wounded, and 150 taken prisoners. Federal loss, 25 killed, 83 wounded and 10 taken prisoners.

December 7. Skirmish near Oakland, Miss. The abolition army commanded by Gen. Hovey and Steele, is repulsed by Whitfield's cavalry, and driven back.

December 7. Claiborne F. Jackson, Governor of Missouri, died near Little Rock, Arkansas.

December 7. The Yankee transport Lake City captured at Carson's Landing, Mississippi river.

December 7. Battle of Hartsville, Tenn. Gen. Morgan accomplishes a most brilliant victory over the abolitionists, defeating them and taking two entire regiments. Federal loss, 100 killed, 500 wounded and 2,000 taken prisoners. Confederate loss 150 killed and wounded.

December 7. Fight at Prestonburg, Ky. Abolitionists defeated and put to route by Col. O'Franklin, 100 ——— ——, 90 killed and wounded, and he succeeds in saving his army. Confederate loss, 4 killed and 9 wounded.

December 7. Battle of Cane Hill, near Boston Mountain, Benton county, Ark. The Confederates, under Gen. Hindman, fought the enemy for two days, winning a decided victory. Federal loss, 1,055 killed and wounded and 240 taken prisoners. Confederate loss, 1,500 killed and wounded and 28 taken prisoners.

December 8. Gen. Floyd surprises the enemy at Charleston, Ky., and captures the place; over 100 Yankees killed; large amount of stores captured.

December 10. Battle of Plymouth, North Carolina. The federals defeated and driven from the town, 25 taken prisoners. Confederate loss, 7 wounded.

December 12. The Federal iron-clad ram Cairo, the flagboat of the Yankee fleet, was blown up by torpedoes, in the Yazoo river, Mississippi. Over 100 lives lost.

December 11. The Yankees repulsed in their first attempt to cross the Rappahannock.

December 12. Skirmish near Kingston, N. C. Confederates defeated.

December 12. Fight at Joyner's Ford, Blackwater river,

Va. Confederate cavalry surprised and 35 captured prisoners.

December 13. Skirmish at Ellis' Ferry, Va. Abolitionists routed with heavy loss.

December 11. Skirmish near Tuscumbia, Ala. Confederates repulsed, and 20 killed and wounded. Federal loss, 30 killed and wounded.

December 13, 14. Battle of Fredericksburg, Va. In this, the most bloody battle of the war, the federal army under Gen. Burnside, was most signally repulsed and defeated by Gen. Lee. Federal loss, 2,000 killed, 8,500 wounded, and 1,626 taken prisoners. Confederate loss, 400 killed, 2,500 wounded, and 476 missing. Generals Cobb and Gregg killed, of the Confederates.

The Yankee attempts to capture Richmond, now numbering four, have cost them at least 125,000 men. Beginning with the first Manassas battle, and going through McClellan's fatal campaign in the Peninsula, Jackson's week of fighting in the Valley, Lee's hurling back of the Pope expedition, including the second battle of Manassas, and now the slaughter on the Rappahannock, we have an amount of carnage that ought to satisfy even Black Republicans.

December 13, 14. Battle of Kingston, N. C. Confederates repulsed, and fell back before an overwhelming force.

December 16. Battle of Whitehall, N. C. Confederates defeated. After occupying Kingston for a short time, the Federals evacuated the place, which was again taken possession of by the Confederates. Federal loss, 1,200 killed and wounded. Total Confederate loss in the several battles was 71 killed, 286 wounded, and 400 missing.

December 12, 16. President Davis visits Tennessee and Mississippi.

December 15, 16. Gen. Burnside re-crosses the Rappahannock river, Va., under cover of night, after the desperate battle of Fredericksburg.

December 16. Gen. Banks, with 8,000 men, arrives at New Orleans, La., and supercedes the "Brute Butler," who is sent North.

December 17. Battle near Goldsboro, N. C. The Federals repulsed, and driven back after a severe engagement.

December 18. Gen. Lovel is removed from the Army of the West, and sent to Virginia. Gen. Loring takes his place. Gen. Van Dorn is appointed to take command of the cavalry forces in the West.

December 18, 19. Gen. Grant's abolition army falls back from Mississippi.

December 18. Brigadier General J. K. Duncan died in Knoxville, Tenn.

December 17, 18. Gen. Forrest annoys the Federals in West Tennessee, destroys railroad bridges and federal property, and captures several towns in his successful raids.

December 18. Skirmish at Lexington, Tenn. Gen. Forrest surprised the Yankees; a sharp fight took place in which 400 of the enemy were killed and wounded. Confederate loss 120 killed and wounded.

December —. Van Buren, Arkansas, captured by the federals. Large amounts of confederate property destroyed.

December 20. The Thirty-Eighth Georgia Regiment numbered 1,100 men when they left home for the War in Virginia. They lost in killed and wounded 56? men (not counting those having died from sickness and disease) in the various battles in which they have been engaged.

December 20. Yankee transports fired on near Newbern, N. C.; fifty killed and wounded. Gen. Wheeler drives in the Yankee pickets at Newbern.

December 20. A large force of abolitionists under Gen. Milroy, are devastating the country in the Virginia valley. Confederate property seized. People maltreated.

December 20. Great trouble in the Lincoln Cabinet at Washington. Seward threatens to resign. The Yankee papers admit the slaughter of their men at Fredericksburg to be unparalleled.

December 21. Gen. Van Dorn surprises the Yankee garrison at Holly Springs, and captures the place after a brisk fight. One thousand nine hundred and fifty Yankees taken prisoners. $6,000,000 worth of Federal stores and property destroyed by the confederates. Federal loss, 350 killed and wounded. Confederate loss, 15 killed and wounded.

December 21. Fight on the Franklin Pike, Tenn. Federals routed with considerable loss. Confederate loss, 2 killed and 6 wounded.

December 21. Skirmish at Davis Mills, Miss. Gen. Van Dorn's cavalry engages the yankees; after a severe fight, the confederates were defeated with a loss of 65 killed and wounded. Federal loss, 83 killed and wounded.

December 22. An abolition clearing going on at Isle of Wight Court House, was broken up by the confederates. Several killed on both sides. President Davis issues his roclamation proscribing Butler as a ¶'.on. The yankees commit outrages on the citizens of H*'.ly Springs, on account of Van Dorn's raid into that city.

December 23. Gen. Buckner 'akes command at Mobile, Ala.

December 24. Fighting at Glasgow, Ky. Gen. Morgan routes the enemy, killing a large number. Three confederates killed.

December 24, 25. Gen. Rosencranz with 35,000 men advances from Nashville. Sever skirmishing continues near Lavergne, Tenn. The confederates fall back. A great battle imminent.

December 24, 25. A party of yankees make a successful raid into Louisiana, on the line of the Shreveport and Vicksburg Railroad; they burn bridges and commit depredations in several towns on the Road.

December 26. Gen. J. E. B. Stuart accomplishes another successful raid in the rear of the federal army, destroys large amounts of federal property, and captures 180 prisoners.

December 26, 27. Heavy skirmishing near Triune and Lavergne, Tenn.

December 27. Attack on the batteries at Snyder's Bluff, Yazoo river; the yankee gunboats repulsed; 11 yankees killed; confederate loss, 1 killed and 7 wounded.

December 26. The federals land a large force at Baton Rouge, La. Gen. Banks establishes his headquarters there.

The yankees burn the State House and destroy all confederate property. Skirmishing on the Yazoo River, Miss. Yankees repulsed and driven to their gunboats.

December 25, 27, 28. Gen. Wheeler's cavalry makes several successful attacks on the rear of Rosencranz's army; 700 yankees captured; large amounts of federal stores destroyed; several confederates killed and wounded.

December 27. Fight at Bloomfield Mo.; a party of confederate guerillas routed by a large force of yankees, and 50 captured.

December 27. Gen. Morgan made a successful raid into Elizabethtown, Tenn., and captured 600 prisoners; and destroyed a large amount of federal property.

December 28, 29, 30. Battle of Chickasaw Bayou, near Vicksburg, Miss. The yankees most signally defeated and put to route after three days' hard fighting. Enemy's loss, 500 killed, and wounded, and 400 taken prisoners. Confederate loss, 170 killed and wounded.

December 29. A large force of yankee cavalry make a successful raid into East Tennessee, destroyed several bridges. Fight at Wat uga Bridge, Tenn. Confederates surprised, and 112 men captured by the enemy; several killed and wounded on both sides. .

December 29. The federals repulsed and driven from Van Buren, Ark., with a loss of 60 killed and wounded.

December 29. Skirmish at Baton Rouge, La.; confederates repulsed.

December 30. The great federal gunboat Monitor foundered at sea and 40 lives lost.

December 31. Battle at Parker's Cross Roads, Tenn.; Gen. Forrest had a desperate fight with the enemy, who surrounded his small force; he succeeded in cutting his way out with a loss of 60 killed, 189 wounded, and 250 taken prisoners.

December 31—January 1, 2, 1863. Battle of Murfreesboro, Tenn.; skirmishing a a prelude to the great battle commenced on December 27; the confederate forces under Gen. Bragg numbered 34,000; the federal forces under Gen. Rosencrantz numbered 50.000 men; the hardest fight took place on the 31st, when the enemy were repulsed and driven from the field with heavy loss; the confederates captured 6,000 stand of arms and 23 cannon, and took 5,000 prisoners; the most bloody and desperate fight took place on January 2d, when Gen. Breckinridge's division attempted to capture one of the enemy's fortified points on Stone River; Gen. Breckinridge was repulsed with terrible slaughter; on January 3d, Gen. Bragg fell back to Shelbyville and Tullahoma, and carried off all the spoils and prisoners; confederate loss, 9,000 killed and wounded and 1,200 taken prisoners; federal loss, 16,940 killed and wounded and 6,273 taken prisoners.

1863.

January 1st. Engagement at Galveston, Texas; Gen. Magruder defeats the yankees, takes possession of Galveston city, and captures the federal gunboat Harriet Lane, achieving a most signal victory over the enemy. Confederate loss, 20 killed and 30 wounded. Federal loss, 163 killed and 200 wounded, and 200 taken prisoners. The yankees blew up two of their boats to prevent their being captured.

January 2. Fighting at Jonesville, Va.; Gen. Marshall engages the federals and drives them from the town.

January 6. Fighting at Boston Mountain, Ark.; a band

of bushwheckers and yankees defeated; 12 killed and 27 taken prisoners.

January 8. Battle of Springfield Mo.; the confederates attacked the place and were repulsed with a loss of 20 killed and 82 wounded.

January 9. Skirmish at Sommerville, Tenn.; 8 confederates captured.

January 9, '10. Battle at Arkansas Post, Arkansas river, Ark; the federals attacked the place with a fleet of gunboats and a heavy land force; after two days hard fighting the confederates surrendered. Federal loss, 1,500 killed and wounded. Confederate loss 150 killed and 600 wounded, and 3,760 taken prisoners.

January 10. Battle at Hartville, Mo.; the yankees repulsed by Gen. Marmaduke, with a loss of 13 killed and 47 wounded. Confederate loss, 15 killed and 70 wounded.

January 11. Skirmish near Clarendon, Ark.; 13 yankees killed and wounded.

January 11. Naval fight in Galveston Bay, Texas; the federal war steamer Hatteras sunk by the privateer Alabama.

January 13. The confederate steamer Princess Royal with a valuable cargo, captured while attempting to run the blockade fleet off Charleston, South Carolina.

January 13. Gen. Forrest had a brisk fight with the yankees at Saulsbury, Va., defeating them with heavy loss.

January 14. Battle at Teche, Bayou Teche, La.; the yankees defeated with a loss of 150 killed and wounded. Confederate loss, 17 killed, 103 wounded.

January 15. Gen. Forrest attacks and destroys several yards steamboats at Cumberland River, Tenn.

January 16. The confederate steamer Florida (Oreta) runs through the blockading fleet from Mobile, Ala.

OPERATIONS IN ARKANSAS AND MISSOURI.

Batesville, Ark., Jan. 13, 1863.

In obedience to instructions from Major General Hindman, I marched from Lewisburg, Ark., December 31, 1862, via Yellville, Ark., so as to reach the enemy in "rear and flank," with 1,000 cavalry and two guns, and 350 of a under McDonald. Before starting I telegraphed to Lieut. Gen. Holmes if it would not be well to move up the troops under Col. White to co-operate in the movement, to which he consented, and the order was given. Col. Porter, with 600 men moved forward for this purpose.

En route in the Boston mountains, Shelby attacked sixty tories and deserters—killed twelve and captured twenty-seven. McDonald surprised, captured - and burned Fort Lawrence, on Beaver creek, Mo. ; of its garrison killed ten, captured seventeen, and routed the rest—about. 258 —captured 200 horses, 300 stand of arms, ten wagons and a quantity of quartermaster and commissary stores.

Shelby captured and burnt the Fort at Ozark. The garrison fled. With Shelby and McDonald I attacked Springfield, Mo., and after eight hours' hard fighting, driving the Yankees before me and into their strongholds, I captured one piece of artillery, (6 pounder.) a stockade fort, a large part of the town, which the yankees burnt as they retired. At dark the fighting ceased—the greater part of the federals in my possession. The federal force there was 4,200. My loss was 20 killed and 80 wounded. The yankee loss was much greater. I did not deem it best to renew the attack, and the next day marched toward Rolla. The federals scattered and fled before me. I burnt the forts at Sand Springs and Marshfield. After passing through Marshfield formed a junction with Porter, who had burnt the forts at Hartsville and Hazlewood.

All the forts burnt were well built works, generally large "block houses," with stockade and good earthworks around, so strong that 100 brave men well armed could defy a thousand infantry or cavalry.

After joining Porter I marched south easterly, making my way toward Arkansas. At Hartsville I met, fought and drove in the direction of Lebanon 1,600 infantry and 500 cavalry, under Gen. Merrill. The battle was desperate. My loss was 15 killed and 70 wounded ; of the former was the brave McDonald, Lt. Col. Weimer, Maj. Kettley, and other brave officers and men. The federal loss was also heavy. The enemy sent in a flag to bury their dead. At this place I captured a caisson with ammunition, a number of small arms, and about 150 great coats, which the Yankees left as they ran off.   J. S. MARMADUKE,
                    Brigadier-General Commanding.

January 21. Engagement in Galveston Bay, Texas; two federal vessels, "Morning Light" and "Velocity" with their crews captured near Sabine Pass.

Jan'y 22. Skirmish near Carthage, La; the federals routed with a loss of 15 killed. Appearance of federals in force opposite Vicksburg, Mississippi; the third siege of the city commences.

Jan. 26. Fight near Athens, Ky; several killed on both sides,

January 27. Bombardment of Fort McAllister, Ga; the yankee fleet repulsed and driven off; no injury sustained at the Fort. Gen'l Burnside resigns command of the federal army of the Potomac, and is succeeded by Gen'l Hooker, Skirmish at Bloomfield, Missouri; confederates defeated and 50 taken prisoners.

January 20. Fight near Murfreesboro, Tenn; federals repulsed with a loss of 200 killed and wounded, Battle at Kelly's store, near Suffolk, Va; the yankees under General Corcoran defeated by Gen'l Pryor; federal loss 700 killed and wounded, confederate loss 18 killed and 45 wounded.

January 31. The confederate gunboats Chicora and Palmetto State make a successful attack on the yankee blockading fleet at Charleston, South Carolina; three of the yankee vessels were badly damaged, and the blockade broken for a time; federal loss 50 killed and 70 wounded, confederate loss none. Fighting at Richmond, Louisiana; after shelling the town, the yankees retired with a loss of 8 killed.

January 30. The yankee congress passes an act to receive negroes into the federal army.

February 2. The federal gunboat Queen of the West runs past the batteries at Vicksburg, Miss.

February 3. Skirmish at McMinnville, Tennessee; federals routed and 30 taken prisoners. Fight at Fort Donelson, Tennessee; the confederates under General Wheeler attack the fort, and after a desperate fight the confederates were repulsed with a loss of 108 killed and wounded, and 200 taken prisoners; federal loss 14 killed, 37 wounded, and 75 captured.

February 2, 3. Skirmishing near Murfreesboro, Tennessee. Fighting near Lake One, Louisiana; yankees repulsed with a loss of 8 killed.

February 7. Skirmish near Williamsburg, Virginia; yankees defeated with a loss of 7 killed and wounded, and 36 taken prisoners.

February 10, 15. The yankee army in Arkansas continues their tyrannical and plundering mode of warfare; cities and towns sacked, the people imprisoned and robbed, outrages of all descriptions committed.

February 13. Two companies of confederates surprised and captured near Kingston, North Carolina. The federal iron clad gunboats run past the batteries at Vicksburg. Miss.

February 13. A sharp skirmish took place near Nolansville, Tennessee; several killed on both sides.

February, 14. Lieutenant Colonel Wood, a confederate prisoner in Memphis, Tennessee, brutally murdered by a yankee soldier.

February '6. Skirmish near Romrey, Virginia; yankees routed and 72 taken prisoners,

February 19, 20. Bombarding at Vicksburg, Mississippi, by the yankee fleet.

February — Skirmish near Strausburg, Virginia; 200 yankees killed and wounded.

February 20. The yankee forces at Vicksburg commence making another canal, "the Bayou Macon and Lake Providence canal scheme," to pass Vicksburg in safety.

February 20. Skirmish near Lake Providence, Louisiana; the federals defeated with a loss of 10 killed and 20 wounded.

February — Clifton on the Tennessee river destroyed by yankee gunboats, 40 confederates captured.

February 21. Engagement at Fort Lowry, Rappahannock river, Virginia; the enemy's boats repulsed; seven yankees killed.

February 22. Federal cavalry raid into Tuscumbia, Ala; the enemy do great damage to the town.

February 24. The federal gunboat Indianola, which succeeded in running the gauntlet at Vicksburg, was captured in a sinking condition after a desperate fight near New Carthage, Louisiana, by confederate gunboats; federal loss 18 killed and wounded and 120 taken prisoners; confederate loss 8 killed and wounded.

February 25. Gen'l Fitzhugh Lee makes a dash into the federal lines near Hartwood Church, Virginia, and creates great havoc among the yankees, killing 76 and capturing 150 prisoners; confederate loss 16 killed and wounded. Two federal gunboats repulsed at Fort Lee, Rappahannock river, Va.

February 24, 25. Bombardment at Galveston, Texas.

February 26. Gen'l Jones attacks the yankees near Brentwood church, Virginia, and puts them to rout, capturing 200 prisoners; confederate loss 7 killed and wounded.

February — A small force of confederates under Major White crosses the Potomac near Poolsville, Maryland, and engages the yankees successfully, and took 17 prisoners.

February — Captain Randolph, of Black Horse cavalry,

*makes several successful raids into the enemy's lines and cap-
tures in all 200 yankees.

February 28, The federal gunboats make another attack
on Fort McAllister, Georgia; the fleet retires without doing
any damage to the fort. The confederate steamer Nashville
(Rattlesnake) destroyed by the enemy on Ogeechee river, Ga,
while attempting to run the blockade.

February 29. Skirmish at Richmond, Louisiana; 5 yankees
killed and wounded,

March 1. Fight at Tuscumbia, Alabama; Gen'l Van Dorn
repulsed, a few of his men captured.

March 2. Skirmish near Bradysville, Tennessee; confederate loss 20 killed and wounded, federal loss 23 killed and
wounded.

March 3. Attack and bombardment of Fort McAllister,
Georgia, resumed, the enemy again repulsed; 2 confederates
wounded; the fort sustained no injury.

March 5. General Toombs resigns his commission in the
confederate army.

March 5. Fight near Kansas city, Missouri, between Quan-
tril's guerilla band and yankee cavalry; yankee loss 9 killed
and wounded. The Great Yazoo Pass expedition, to get in
the rear af Vicksburg, enters Coldwater river. A brisk fight
took place at Mount Sterling, Kentucky, in which the federals
were routed and 50 taken prisoners.

March 6. Skirmishing on Coldwater river, Mississippi; the
yankee gunboats and transports fired on, several of the federals killed.

March 4, 5. Battle of Springhill, near Franklin, Tennessee;
the confederates under General Van Dorn repulses the federals after a severe fight; confederate loss 56 killed and 289
wounded; federal loss 90 killed, 237 wounded, and 2200 taken
prisoners.

March 7. A party of federal cavalry makes a dash into
Winslow, North Carolina, and committed many depredations.
General Jones defeats the federals at Woodstock, Va, killing
and wounding 30 men and took 250 prisoners; confederate loss
12 killed and wounded.

March 8. Several negro (federal) regiments leave Hilton
Head, South Carolina, for Florida, with the intention of exci-
ting an insurrection among the slaves. Colonel Wood surprises the yankees at Liberty, Tennessee, and captures 85 men,
together with a large amount of stores.

March 9. Skirmish near Bolivar, Tennessee. Gen'l Kirby

Smith sent to take command of Trans-Mississippi department, General Price sent to Arkansas in place of Gen'l Hindman, removed.

March 9, 10, A daring and successful raid into the yankee camps at Fairfax Courthouse, Virginia; the yankee General Stoughton and 150 federals taken prisoners; a large amount of federal property destroyed.

March 10, 11. Fight near Jacksonville, Florida; on the 10th the federals landed a force of 1400 negroes and garrisoned the place; on the 11th the confederates attacked the place and killed a large number of the yankee (negroes).

March 11, 12. Yankee cavalry makes a raid into the confederate lines near Murfreesboro', Tenn., and captures 114 men. Gen. Van Dorn's command retreats successfully across Duck River, Tenn.; during the retreat several fights took place, in which the Yankees were kept at bay.

March 11. The Yankees attempt to capture a confederate steamer engaged in the blockade trade, at Smyrna, Fla; the captain and crew of the boat attacked and drove off the yankees, killing and wounding 20.

March 12. Fighting in Clark county, Ark. A large party of yankees and jayhawkers defeated and driven from the county.

March 11, 12, 13. Battle of the Yazoo, Tallahatchie, Miss. The yankee fleet attacks Fort Pemberton; after some hard fighting, the enemy was severely repulsed and driven off—confederate loss 11 killed and wounded; fed.ral loss 10 killed and wounded.

March 13, 14. Gen. Banks advances towards Port Hudson, La., and is compelled to fall back, after several unsuccessful skirmishes.

March 13 The federals admit that 100 men die daily from sickness from their army before Vicksburg, Miss. Skirmishing at Deep Gully, Nor. Car. General Hill repulsed by the federals with a loss of 24 killed and wounded.

March 14, 15. The persevering yankees try another route to get in the rear of Vicksburg, by the Deer Creek and Sunflower rivers, Miss. A democratic newspaper office destroyed by federal soldiers at Richmond, Indiana. Naval attack on Port Hudson, La; a great battle took place in which the yankee fleet was badly worsted—two steamers disabled and the frigate Mississippi burned; only two steamers passed the batteries, the Hartford and Albatross: federal loss estimated at 260 killed and wounded, confederate loss only three wounded.

March 15. The N. Y. Herald in a recent summing up of "the profit and loss account of Secretary-Wells' administration," makes the following admissions with respect to the prowess of our little cruisers :

"The amount of Northern property destroyed at sea by the rebel cruisers and privateers Alabama, Florida, Retribution, Sumter, Jeff. Davis, &c., may be estimated at from ten to fifteen million dollars. The damage inflicted on our commerce by the panic created by these losses it would not be easy to calculate. This, whatever it may be, will be increased ten fold by the destruction of the Jacob Bell, with her valuable cargo of from a million to a million and a half of dollars. The consternation occasioned by it will have the effect of taking out of our hands all our East India trade and throwing it into those of Great Britain—an object for which she has long been covetous.

"According to a statement made by Mr. Grimes in the Senate, we have captured at sea, prizes to the amount of about fifteen millions of dollars—those in New York being valued at more than half that sum. The proceeds of these go to a few persons, being divided among our naval officers and sailors, a portion only falling to the share of the government. This is no offset to the losses that we have been sustaining by the activity of the rebel privateers. With a navy of more than four hundred vessels, we have, notwithstanding the immense number of ships that have sailed from England for rebel ports within the last two years, effected seizures to the amount of only fifteen millions of dollars. The game, it must be admitted, is a costly one, and the gains are almost entirely on one side."

March 16. Battle of Yazoo, Tallahatchie, Miss Fighting again resumed ; the Yankees again defeated, two of their gunboats disabled—confederate loss during the siege of Fort Pemberton 3 killed and 20 wounded. Skirmish near Jacksonville, Fla—the federals defeated.

March 16, 17. Battle at Kelley's Ford, Rappahannock river, Va. The Federals in attempting to cross the river were most signally defeated after a desperate fight—confederate loss 250 killed and wounded and 50 taken prisoners ; the gallant Maj. Pelham killed ; yankee loss very heavy. Yankees commit depredations at Fernando, Miss.; they are driven off by Col. Blythe's cavalry. Yankee cavalry makes a charge on a confederate battery on the Blackwater river, Va., and met with a severe repulse.

March 19. Battle near Milton, Tenn. Gen'l J. H. Morgan had a severe fight with the Yankees, in which he was compelled to fall back with a loss of 24 killed and 120 wounded.

March 21, 22. The yankees who have occupied Pensacola, Fla., evacuated the city; before leaving they set fire to the city in many places, doing great damage.

March — Reported fight at Hazel Green, Ky. Federals defeated with a loss of 36 killed.

March 21. Col. Clarke captures Mount Sterling, Ky., and took 200 yankee prisoners.

March 22. Captain Ferrill makes a successful dash into the enemy's lines near Occaquon river, Va., and captures several prisoners. The new confederate cotton loan has been more than successful in London and Paris, commanding a premium of 4½ per cent.

Loss of Yankee Generals.—In a recent debate in the Yankee senate, Wilson stated that they had lost twenty-six general officers since the war commenced, seventeen of whom were killed in battle.

March 24. Skirmish at Rienzi, Miss.; three companies of yankees surprised and 11 captured by partizan rangers.

March 21, 22. Skirmishing on Sunflower river, Miss. The great yankee expedition to Deer creek and Sunflower rivers is defeated and driven back; several of their gunboats disabled.

March 23, 25. Fight at Pontchatoula, La; the yankees attacked and captured the town; they were afterwards defeated and driven from the town, with a loss of 30 killed and wounded—confederate loss 11 wounded. Four federal boats run the gauntlet at Vicksburg, two of them sunk and one disabled.

March — Fighting at Ripley, Miss; the yankees worsted and driven from the town.

March 25. A force of 600 yankees while crossing the Amite river, La, were fired on by Bryan's scouting party and 27 killed and many were drowned. Gen'l Forrest surprises the yankee garrison at Brentwood, Tenn, and took 750 prisoners and destroyed a large amount of federal property; confederate loss 7 killed and 35 wounded; federal loss 16 killed, 10 wounded. Danville, Ky, captured by the confederates; the yankees fled precipitately, with some killed and wounded.

March 26. Fight at Lancaster, Ky, Gen'l Pegram routes the federals and captured many prisoners.

March 27. A yankee gunboat attacked on St John's river, Fla, and several of the crew killed. Fight in Oclockney Bay, Fla, and yankees defeated—the notorious federal "Jim Montgomery" killed.

March 28, 29. The yankee negro regiments who occupied the town of Jacksonville, Fla, evacuated the place after firing the town and destroying the larger portion of the place; several skirmishes occurred while the enemy held the town.

March 28. A severe thunder storm passes over Vicksburg, Miss, during which 10 soldiers were killed and 16 wounded by the falling of trees on their camps.

March 28. Yankee raid into McNutt, Miss, they steal a large amount of property. Attack on Moscow, Tenn, by partizan

rangers; 10 yankees killed and considerable property destroy·
ed. Major Tabb makes a successful dash into Williamsburg,
Va, killing and capturing several of the enemy. Naval fight in
Berwick's Bay, La; the federal gunboat Diana captured; fede·
ral loss 10 killed, 20 wounded and 98 taken prisoners. Some
excitement created by outbreaks headed by women, "called
women's bread riots" in several cities in the confederacy.

*March 29.· A negro (yankee) regiment at Pilatka, Fla, were
surprised and 30 killed and wounded.

March 30. Fight near Woodbury, Tenn. Federal loss 22
killed and 50 wounded; confederate loss 22 killed and 67
wounded.

March 30, 31. Skirmishing near Unionville, Tenn; the yan·
kees defeated in several engagements by Wharton's Texan
rangers. Battle near Somersett, Ky; the confederates under
Gen'l Pegram met with a severe repulse; confederate loss 200
killed and wounded, and 150 taken prisoners; federal loss
130 killed and wounded.

March 30. Colonel Jenkins' cavalry makes a dash into Point
Pleasant, Va, and puts the yankee garrison to route, killing
many, a large amount of yankee stores destroyed.

March 31. Bursting of a cannon at Grand Gulf, Miss, two
confederates killed and 8 wounded. Great outrages, murder
and robbery committed by jayhawkers near Fort Scott, Mo.
Colonel Mosby makes a successful dash into the yankee camps
at Centreville, Va, surprises the enemy, killing and wounding
thirty.

April 1. Gunboat attack on Tuscumbia, Ala; the yankees
repulsed with heavy loss. Skirmish at Drainsville, Va; the
yankees routed with a loss of 60 killed and 79 taken prisoners.

April 2. Two yankee gunboats damaged by a confederate
battery at Palmyra, (Tenn) river; the enemy afterwards burn·
ed the town.

April 2. Skirmish near Antioch, Ten; Major McCann cap·
tures a train of cars; 42 yankees killed and 67 wounded; con·
federate loss 13 killed and wounded. Outbreak in Richmond,
Va, called "woman's bread riots," under the lead of women;
several stores broken open and goods carried away. A state·
ment in a Liverpool journal gives a list of 38 vessels captured
or destroyed by the steamer Alabama, from February 1st to
March 1st, 1863.

April 3, 4. Battle of Snow Hill near Woodbury, Tenn;
Gen'l Morgan repulses the enemy after a severe fight;·confed·
erate loss 17 killed and wounded; federal loss heavy. The

federal steamer Fox (Whittemore) captured near mouth of Mississippi river, by confederates, and successfully brought into a confederate port.

April 4, 5. Skirmishing near Fort Pemberton, Tallahatchie river, Miss, the yankees fell back, abandoning the Yazoo Pass expedition route. Yankees repulsed at Bay Port, Fl., .

April 7. Naval battle in Charleston harbor, South Carolina; the yankee fleet of monitors and iron clads, under Commodore Dupont, attacks the forts near Charleston, and after a sharp engagement the fleet was repulsed and driven off; all vessels of the fleet were damaged, the monitor Keokuk sunk; federal loss 15 killed and wounded, confederate loss 4 killed and 8 wounded; the confederate forts sustained no material injury. Bombarding at Port Hudson, La.

April 7. Skirmish at Greenhill, Tenn; several killed on both sides.   •

April 7. A yankee gunboat destroyed by a confederate battery on Coosa river, S C; 7 yankees killed and wounded.

April 7, 8, 9. Siege of Washington, N C, by the confederates under Gen'l Hill; on the 10th instant a brisk skirmish took place in which the enemy were defeated.

April 9. Fight at New Carthage, La; 7 yankees killed and wounded. Fight at Pascagoula, Miss; a large force of federals (yankees and negroes) effects a landing in town; after a brisk fight they are driven off with a loss of 5 killed and a large number wounded. Gold sold at 500 per centum premium in Richmond, Va.

April 10. The execution of the notorious Federal spy and jayhawker, Captain A C Webster, by the confederate authorities in Richmond, Va. A railroad train attacked near Lavergne, Tenn, by Gen'l Wheeler; 60 yankees killed and 20 captured.

April 9, 10 Battle at Franklin, Tenn; Gen'l Van Dorn attacked the enemy and was defeated after a most bloody and desperate fight; confederate loss 100 killed and wounded and 30 taken prisoners, federal loss 60 killed and wounded.

April 11. Battle and capture of Williamsburg, Va, by Gen Wise. Col Tabb gets in the rear of the yankees at Fort McGruder, Va, and whips the enemy. Skirmish on the Tennessee and Mississippi railroad, Miss; federals repulsed with a loss of 60 killed and wounded.

April 10. A daring raid by confederates into the enemy's lines on the Nashville and Murfreesboro railroad, Tenn; 75 yankees killed and wounded. It is estimated that the confederate debt on the first of July, 1863, will amount to $900,000,-000, fifteen per centum of all the property in the Confederate States.

April 11, 12, 13. Battles of Camp Bisland, Bayou Teche country, La; the confederates defeated in several severe fights and driven from all their positions, by Gen'l Banks; five confederate steamers burned, and two gunboats destroyed, with a large amount of confederate stores; confederate loss 1000 killed, wounded and prisoners; federal loss 7,834. Siege of Suffolk, Va; Gen'l Longstreet defeats tho yankees in several engagements near the city; two federal gunboats disabled on the Nansemond river, Va.

April 12, 13. Evacuation of Cole's Island by the yankees, who were to capture Charleston; some skirmishing took place during the retreat.

April 12. Bursting of an English Whitworth gun in a confederato battery near Washington, North Carolina; 8 killed.

April 13. Two Federal gunboats disabled on Nansemond river, Va.; 23 yankees killed.

April 14. Skirmish at Kelley's Ford, Va. The federals while attempting to cross the Rappahannock river, Va., are repulsed, with a loss of 25 killed and wounded.

April — Federal bushwackers hung ; a father and son executed in Ashe county, North Carolina.

April 15. Major Harrison has a skirmish with the yankees at New Carthage, La.; 5 of the enemy killed.

April 17, 19. Fighting near Tuscumbia, Ala. Col. Roddy engaged the enemy with varying success ; captured 100 prisoners, and fell back across Big Bear Creek; confederate loss 17 killed and wounded. Fight at Laurel Ridge, North Carolina; yankees repulsed ; confederate loss 9 killed and wounded. A new yankee battery on the point opposite Vicksburg commences shelling the city. The confederate steamer Stonewall Jackson sunk by the blockaders off Charleston, South Carolina. Skirmishing near Big Bear creek, Ala. The confederates capture 170 yankees ; confederate loss 26 killed and wounded. Brig Gen. D. S. Donelson died at Montvale Springs, Tenn.

April 18. Yan'ee gunboat captured in Sabine Pass, Texas.

April 18, 19. Fighting at Cold Water, Miss. Col. Blythe routes the enemy ; 17 yankees killed and 50 wounded ; confederate loss 3 killed and 8 wounded ; the federal Major Mayos killed.

April 18. Confederates defeated near Elizabeth city, North Carolina, with a loss of 6 killed and 31 wounded.

—— Gen. Wheeler makes a successful raid into Cartsville, Tenn., and took 100 yankee prisoners.

April 18. Battle at Fayetteville, Ark. ; confederates defeated with a loss of 22 killed and wounded.

April 19. •Skirmishing near Suffolk, Va. ; 50 confederates captured by the yankees. •

April 20 Fighting at Patterson, Mo. Gen'l Marmaduke routes the enemy and captures the town ; yankee loss 68 killed and wounded. The town of Celina, Tenn., burned by the yankees ; a large lot of confederate stores destroyed ; confederate loss 90 killed and wounded ; federal loss 28 killed and wounded. The confederates advance into South-west Missouri. Fight near Pilot Knob ; yankees defeated, with a loss of 75 killed and wounded.

April 21. 1♠n. W. H. Cook, of Missouri, died in Petersburg, Va. Yankes raid into McMinville, Tenn. ; confederates surprised, and 100 taken prisoners ; narrow escape of Gen, •Morgan and Major McCann ; the enemy do great damage to the town.

April 22, 23. Gen'l Ellet's (yankee) Marine Brigade destroys several towns on the Tennessee river, Tenn. ; the fleet, fired on by a confederate battery, 10 yankees killed. Yankee raid into Woodstock, Va ; the town robbed and plundered, several citizens wounded.

April 24. Yankee raid into Port Royal, Va.; confederate property destroyed. Fighting at Beverly, Western Virginia. Gen'l Imboden attacks the yankees and drives them from their position ; a large amount of federal stores destroyed. The most daring and successful raid of the war Three regiments, (1,500 men) of federal cavalry, with six pieces of artillery, under command of Col. Grierson, started from LaGrange, Tenn., on the 17th of April, and advances through Mississippi, and arrives successfully at Baton Rouge, -La. The raiders travelled over 800 miles in seventeen days, and committed great depredations on private and public property, destroyed the principal southern railroads in many places, burned several towns in Mississippi. Several skirmishes occurred in their travels in which the raiders were successful ; their loss was only 2 killed and 9 wounded. Skirmish at Birmingham, Miss. ; yankees repulsed, with 33 killed and wounded ; confederate loss 22 killed and wounded

April 25, 26. Fighting near Cape Girardeau, Mo. Gen'l Marmaduke attacked the enemy's positions, and was repulsed, with a loss of 50 killed and 180 wounded; federal loss 50 killed and wounded.

April 27. Confederates attack a train of cars on the Louisville and Nashville railroad, and are driven off, with a loss of 9 killed and wounded; federal loss 7 killed and wounded.

April 27. 130 confederates captured by yankee cavalry near Franklin, Tenn.

April 25, 27. Confederates raid into Western Virginia; several bridges destroyed on the Baltimore and Ohio railroad. Skirmish near Jackson, Mo.; confederates routed by Gen'l McNeil.

April 28. Fight near Mill Spring, Ky. The federal war steamer Preble burned off Pensacola, Fla.

April 29. Bombardment at Grand Gulf. Miss. The federal fleet repulsed after a hard fight; confederate loss 18 killed and wounded. Some of the yankee boats disabled; a part of the fleet afterwards succeed in passing by the batteries and land troops below the town. Fighting at Union Church, Miss. Fighting at Hamilton Crossing, Rappahannock river, Va.; the advance of Hooker's yankee army crosses the river; confederate loss 39 killed and wounded and 55 captured.

April 28, 29. Fighting near Kingston, North Carolina; the yankees routed with a loss of 70 killed and wounded; confederate loss 22 killed and wounded.

April 30, May 1, 2. Federal cavalry raid under Col. Streight, into Northern Alabama and Georgia. They do considerable damage in several towns, Gen'l Forrest goes in pursuit of them, and has sharp fights with the marauders, and finally captures the whole command at Cedar Bluff, Ga.; over 100 of the enemy killed and wounded; confederate loss 20 killed and wounded.

April 30. Yankee gunboat attack on Snyder's Bluff, Miss.; the fleet repulsed; two boats disabled; confederate less 3 wounded.

May 1. Fighting at Lewisburg, Va. Col. Edgar signally repulsed the Yankees, who were in large force.

It is estimated that the whole amount of property belonging to the people of our Confederate States, which has been destroyed by the yankees, will amount to $20,000,000.

May 1st. Battle of Bayou Peivre or Port Gibson, Miss. Gen. Grant defeats the Confederates under Gen. Bowen. Confederate loss 670 killed and wounded. Federal loss 930 killed and wounded. Fight near LaGrange, Ark., the Yankees routed, with a less of 40 killed and wounded and 47 taken prisoners.

May 2. Skirmishing near Tullahoma, Tenn. Gen. Forrest routes the Yankee cavalry. Col. Eliett's fleet of Yankee boats attacked on Tennessee river, 13 Yankees killed and wounded. Confederate loss 9 killed and wounded.

May 2, 3, 5. Battles of the Rappahannock, (Chancellorsville and the Wilderness) the Yankee army 120,000 strong, under command of Gen. Hooker; defeated by Gen. Lee, whose army numbered 49,890 men. Federal loss 3,600 killed, 16,400 wounded, and 8,000 prisoners : 27 pieces of artillery captured from the enemy with a vast amount of small arms. Confederate loss 2,300 killed, 8 000 wounded, and 4,000 taken prisoners. Gen. Stonewall Jackson accidentally wounded during the fight on the 2nd, by men of his own brigade. A Federal hospital, containing 600 sick was fired by shells and most of the sick perished during the battle. Federal cavalry raid by Gen. Stoneman on the principal railroads leading to Richmond; they destroy bridges, &c. The raiders finally defeated near Louisa Court house, 30 captured. Confederate loss 9 killed.

May 3 A Yankee steamer sunk while passing the batteries at Vicksburg, Miss., her crew captured. Fighting at Aransas Pass, Texas, three Yankee boats fired on and 20 killed.

May 5. Battle at Tupello, Miss, the Confederates under Col. Barton, repulsed after a severe fight, with a loss of 49 killed and wounded and 81 taken prisoners. Federal loss 45 killed and wounded

May 7. Gen. Van Dorn shot dead at his quarters in Springfield, Tenn , by Dr. Peters.

May 10. Lieut. Gen. Thomas J. (Stonewall) Jackson died in Caroline county, Va., from the effects of a wound received in battle of Chancellorsville. Fighting at Port Hudson, La. Confederate loss 3 killed and wounded.

May 12. Battle of Raymond, Miss. The confederates defeated after a most desperate fight, with a loss of 489 killed and wounded Federal loss 520 killed and wounded.

May 12, 13. Skirmishing near Mississippi Springs, Miss. Grant's army advancing towards Jackson, Miss. Gen. Johnson arrives at Jackson, Miss., from Tennessee.

May 14. Gen. Banks evacuates Alexandria, La. Battle and fall of Jackson, Miss.; the confederates withdraw from the city after a sharp contest, the city occupied by Grant's army.

The city partly burned and sacked by the Yankees. Federal loss 300 killed and wounded.

May 15. Jackson, Miss. evacuated by Grant's army.

May 16. Battle of Baker's Creek, or Champion Hill, Miss.. Gen. Pemberton's army defeated by Grant. Gen. Lloyd Tilghman killed. Federal loss 2, 400 killed and wounded. Confederate loss 1,259 killed and wounded and 2000 taken prisoners. Capt. Elliot captures two Yankee steamers on Chesapeake canal, North Carolina.

May 17. Battle of Big Black Bridge, Miss. Gen. Pemberton again defeated. Confederate loss 263 killed and wounded and 3000 taken prisoners. Federal loss 300 killed and wounded. Gen. Pemberton falls back to Vicksburg, Miss.

May — Major Bridges fires on a Yankee transport fleet near Greenville, Miss., 165 of the Yankees killed and a large number wounded.

May 17. Skirmish in Isle of Wight, Ga. Yankees defeated. Confederate loss 5 killed and wounded.

May 18. Richmond, Mo., captured by the confederates.

May 18. The siege of Vicksburg commences, Gen. Grant attacks the city in the rear. A desperate assault was made by Grant on the 22nd, in which the enemy was terribly repulsed with a loss of over 1,000 killed and wounded; another assault was made on the 24th, the enemy again repulsed.

May 19. Snyder's Bluff (or Haines' Bluff) evacuated by the confederates and occupied by the Yankees.

May 20. Skirmish in Yazoo county, 29 Yankees killed.

May 21. Battle of Plains Store, La. Yankees repulsed after a desperate fight. Confederate loss 70 killed and wounded.

May 21. The Yankees occupy Yazoo city, Miss. A large amount of confederate property destroyed on the Yazoo river.

May 22. Gen. Bank's advance on Port Hudson, La.

May 22. Fighting at Gum Swamp, North Carolina. Confederates surprised and routed with a loss of 15 killed and wounded, and 137 captured. Federal loss 8 killed.

May 22. Skirmish near Fosterville, Tenn. Yankees repulsed. Confederate loss 11 killed and wounded and 50 captured.

May 23. Yankee gunboat fired on at Liverpool, Miss. 19 Yankees killed and wounded. Confederate loss 7 killed.

May 26, 27. Fighting near Florence, Ala. Confederates

repulsed ; the Yankees enter the town and destroy stores and factories.

May 26. A Yankee force routed in Ripley county, Miss. 200 killed, wounded and captured.

May 26. Skirmishing near Lebanon, Tenn. The gunboat Cincinnati sunk by the batteries in front of Vicksburg.

May 26. Skirmishing near Alexandria, La. Yankee wagon train captured.

May 27. The siege of Port Hudson continues. A heavy assault was made on the place, in which the enemy was repulsed with a loss of over 3000 killed and wounded, among which a negro regiment was cut to pieces ; several Yankee Generals wounded. Confederate loss 250 killed and wounded.

May 27, 28. Skirmishing in Yaz o county. The Yankees repulsed with a loss of 30 killed and wounded. C. L. Vallandigham arrives at Shelbyville, Tenn. The confederate gunboat Chattahoochee exploded her boiler on the Chattahoochee river, Ga., 16 persons killed and 34 wounded.

May 28, 29. Federal cavalry raid in the Tennessee valley. Major Harrison routes the raiders. Fight near Port Gibson, Ark., 30 Yankees killed.

May 30. Yankee raid at Bolton's, Miss. ; a large amount of cotton destroyed.

May 31. Battle at Brownsville, Miss. Yankees repulsed.

May 31. Fight at Ashwood, La. Yankees driven to their gunboats. Fight near Greenville, Va. Major Mosely defeats the Yankees.

June 2. A Yankee steamer captured and two Yankee vessels burned off the mouth of Mississippi river by Capt. Duke and eighteen adventurous confederates.

June 2. Gen. Burnside attempts to suppress the N. Y. World and Chicago Times, daily newspapers.

June 3, 4. Skirmishing near Millersburg and Murfreesboro, Tenn ; 11 confederates killed and wounded.

June 5. Fight at Clinton, La ; Col. Logan routes the yankee cavalry, and captures 35 ; confederate loss 19 killed and wounded. Gen'l Jenkins drives the yankees from Strausburg, Va., and occupies the city. Fight at Mechanicksburg, Miss ; yankees defeated with heavy loss ; confederate loss 20 killed and wounded. Skirmishing at Warrenton Springs, Va.

June 5. Fight at Franklin, Tennessee ; Gen'l Forrest defeats the yankees ; confederate loss 150 killed and wounded.

June 6, 7. Skirmishing near Fredicksburg, Virginia ; the yankees driven across the river ; confederate loss 14 killed and wounded and 40 captured. Fight at Willilen's Bend, Louisiana; confederates defeated, with a loss of 150 killed and wounded; federal loss 200 killed and wounded.

June 9. Col. L. W. Orton and Lieut. W. G. Peters hung by order of Gen'l Rosencrans, for being discovered as confederate spies at Franklin, Tenn.

June 9, 10. Battle at Brandy Station, Virginia; a desperate cavalry fight, in which the yankees were defeated, with heavy loss; confederate loss 50 killed and 280 wounded, and 153 taken prisoners; Col's Willians and Hampton killed. Fight at Monticello, Kentucky; the confederates under Gen'l Pelham, defeated, with a loss of 37 killed and wounded; federal loss 40 killed and wounded.

June 11. The town of Darien, Georgia, burned by the yankees. Fight at Ashland, Louisiana; yankees routed.

June 10, 11. Engagement at Fort Beauregard, (Harrisonburg) Louisiana; yankee gunboats driven off.

June 13, 14. Fighting at Winchester, Va. Gen. Ewell captures the place, 3,040 yankees taken prisoners. Confederate loss 27 killed and wounded. Yankees surprised at Silver Springs, Tenn, 16 killed. The siege of Port Hudson continues; the yankees repulsed with great loss.

June 15. Martinsburg, Va. captured by the confederates under Gen. Rhodes.

June 16, 17. Gen. Ewell's army crosses the Potomac in Maryland and Pennsylvania. Gen. Jenkin's cavalry occupies Chambersburg, Penn.

June 17, 18. The siege of Vicksburg continues. Cavalry fight at Middleburg, Va. Confederates repulsed after capturing 240 yankees.

June 17. Skirmish near Richmond, La. The yankees driven from Alexandria, Tenn. Naval fight in Warsaw sound, Ga. The iron-clad steamer Atlanta disabled and captured by the yankees. Confederate loss 19 killed and wounded.

June 18. Fight near Knoxville, Tenn. A yankee raiding party defeated with a loss of 40 killed and wounded. Confederate loss 18 killed and wounded.

June 19. Fight near Hernando, Miss. Gen. Chalmers defeats the yankees. Skirmish near Chambersburg, Penn.; the yankees repulsed. Gen. Jenkins' cavalry occupies the town.

June 20. Fight near Mechanicksburg, Miss. Yankees routed with a loss of 65 killed and wounded.

June 20. Fight near Rocky Ford, Miss. Gen. Ruggles routes the yankees and captures 28 prisoners. Fight at Strawberry

Plains, Tenn. Confederate loss 19 killed and wounded. Federal loss 23 killed and wounded.

June 20. Battle of Mud Creek Swamp, near Pontotoc, Miss. Yankees defeated with a loss of 35 killed and wounded.

June 21. Fight opposite Baton Rouge, La. Gen. Taylor routes the Yankees. Cavalry engagement at Upperville, Va. Gen. Stuart defeated with great loss.

June 21. The Brookhaven raiders, 40 men, defeated and captured near Ellisville, Miss. Federal loss 9 killed and wounded.

June 22. Cavalry fight at Bear Creek, Miss. Yankees routed ; 89 killed and wounded. Confederate loss 22 killed and wounded.

June 22. Gen. Lee's army enters Hagerstown, Maryland.

June 23, 4. Fight at Berwick's Bay, La. The place captured by Gen. Magruder. Federal loss 200 killed and wounded, and 1600 captured. Confederate loss 87 killed and wounded. A large amount of Federal stores captured.

June 24, 25. Fighting at Liberty and Hoover Gaps and New Church, Tenn ; the confederates repulsed. Confederate loss 400 killed and wounded, and 2000 missing. Gen. Bragg evacuates Middle Tennessee and falls back to Chattanooga. Gen. Rosecrans advances and occupies the confederate positions at Shelbyville and Tullahoma, Tenn.

June 26. Fighting at Hanover Court House, Va.

June 28. Gen. Hooker resigns command of the Yankee army North, and is succeeded by Gen. G. G. Meade.

June 29, 30. Battle at Hanover, Penn. Gen. Stuart repulsed after a severe contest. Federal loss 39 killed and wounded, and 150 captured ; confederate loss 32 killed and wounded.

June 30. Federal raid on Deckard's station, Tenn.

July 1, 2, 3. Battle of Gettysburg, Penn. Gen. Lee gained decided victories on the first and second day's fight : on the third day both armies withdrew after a terrible engagement. Confederate loss 3 000 killed, 16,000 wounded, and 4,000 missing and captured. Gens. Hood, Trimble, Armistead, Jones, Jenkins and Archer wounded, and Gens. Garnett, Barksdale and Kemper killed. Federal loss 20,000 killed and wounded, and 8,000 captured.

July 2. Fight at Springfield Landing, La. The Yankees routed with a loss of 119 killed and wounded ; confederate loss 17 killed and wounded.

July 3. Gen'l Pemberton surrenders the city of Vicksburg to Gen'l Grant, after a siege of forty-seven days ; hunger and fatigue compelled Gen'l Pemberton to surrender the garrison; confederate loss during the siege 4,700 killed and wounded; federal loss 7,050 killed and wounded. 27,000 confederates captured.

July 3, 4. Battle of Helena, Ark. The confederates under Gen'l Holmes defeated with a loss of 800 killed and wounded, 1,130 captured; federal loss 350 killed and wounded.

July 3. Fight at Burksville, Ky. Gen'l Morgan defeats the yankees

July 4. Fight at Lebanon, Tenn: Gen'l Morgan captures the city.

July 4, 5. Fight at South Anna Bridge, Va. Gen'l D. H. Hill defeats the Yankees. Vice President Stephen's mission to Washington; he is stopped at Fortress Monroe; the yankees not acknowledging his mission.

July — Battle near Lake Providence, La.

July 5. Battle at Williamsport, Md. Gen. Imboden defeats the yankees.

July 5. Skirmish near Algiers, La. 40 confederate cavalry captured.

July 6. Fighting near Freebridge, North Carolina. Williamston, North Carolina, burned by the Yankees. Fight at Williamsport, Maryland; yankee cavalry defeated.

July 7. Two Federal officers in Richmond, Va., drawn by lot to be executed in retaliation for two confederate officers hung by order of Rosencrans in Tenn. Confederate raid near Corinth and Iuka, Miss.

July — Fight at Green River Bridge, Ky. Gen'l Morgan defeated with a loss of 60 killed and wounded.

July 9. Port Hudson, La., surrendered to Gen'l Banks, after a constant siege, day and night, during seven weeks; the garrison numbered 6,265 men under Gen'l Gardner. Confederate loss during the siege was 303 killed and 517 wounded.

July 8. Gen'l Morgan's daring raid with 6,000 men into the enemy's country; he captures Corydon, Indiana, destroys railroad bridges, &c.

July 10. Skirmish on the Sharpsburg Turnpike, Maryland.

July 10 to 16. Battle and second siege of Jackson, Miss. Gen'l Johnston defeated and evacuates the city. Confederate loss 470 killed and wounded. Federal loss 900 killed and wounded.

July 11. Siege of Charleston, South Carolina. The enemy attack Fort Wagner and are repulsed after a desperate fight,

... Gen. Scott defeats the yankees ...

... May 11.

... killed and ...

... burn ...

... July ... Yankee railroad ... raiders returned.

August —, Fight at Jackson, La. ; Col. Logan ——— yankees.

August 5. Gunboat fight at Chapin's Bluff, James River; the yankees ———

August 10, 11. Skirmish near Brandy Station, Va. ; the yankees surprised and routed, with a loss of 20 killed and wounded.

August 12. The Federal steamer Vanderbilt sunk off the Brazil coast by the confederate steamer Georgia, under command of Capt. Semmes.

August 17. Fight at Sparta, Tenn. ; yankees routed with loss of 35 killed and wounded; confederate loss 23 killed and wounded.

August 17, 18. Terrific bombardment of Fort Sumter and Battery Wagner. Yankee raid on the Mississippi Central railroad, Miss. ; a large number of locomotives and cars destroyed and burned.

August 20, Quantrell's raid on Lawrence, Kansas Territory ; yankee property destroyed ; 180 abolitionists killed and wounded.

August 21. Bombardment of Chattanooga, Tenn. ; 9 persons killed.

August 22. Bombardment of Charleston, South Carolina. Three yankee vessels captured near mouth of Rappahannock river, Va. ; 60 yankees taken prisoners.

August 23, 24. Skirmish near Bristol and Hot Springs.

August 25. Yankee raid into King George; the enemy defeated, with a loss of 17 killed and wounded.

August 26. Gen'l J. B. Floyd died at Abingdon, Va.

August —. Reported defeat of the yankees on White Ark. ; Gen. Price reported successful in Arkansas.

Aug. 21. Battle of White Sulphur Springs, Va. ; yankees defeated with a loss of 300 killed and wounded ; confederate loss 170 killed and wounded.

August 27. Skirmish at big creek, Greenbrier county, Va. ; the yankees repulsed ; confederate loss 130 killed and wounded. Yankee raid at Bottom's Bridge, near Richmond, Va. ; the raiders repulsed.

August —. Gen. M. Jeff Thompson and Capt. Kay captured by the yankees at Pocahontas, Ark.

Sept. 6. Capture of Battery Wagner and Morris Island by the yankees.

Sept. 8. Evacuation of Chattanooga by confederates.

_____ of Fort Sumter, S. C. _____ _____

Sept. 8. Two newspaper _____ _____ _____ _____ and _____ Raleigh, N. C.

Sept. 8-9. Skirmishing near _____ _____ _____ _____ Bragg's troops _____ _____ _____ _____ Railroad. Cumberland Gap surrendered by the _____ _____ _____ Gen. Frazer without resistance. _____ Confederates taken prisoners.

Sept. 11-12. _____ _____ _____ Tenn. 300 Yankees captured. _____ _____ recaptured the _____.

Sept. 12-13. _____ _____ near _____ Court House, Va. Confederates _____ with a loss of _____ killed and wounded. Gen. Stuart defeated _____ _____ Station, Va.

Sept. 12. _____ of _____ _____ _____ Gun at Charleston, S. C.

Sept. 10. _____ near Jonesboro', _____ u. Gen. Buckner drove the Yankees and captured 300 _____ Skirmishing at Kelton Ford, Va. _____ Yankees _____.

Sept. 17. _____ _____ _____ _____ _____

Sept. 18-20. _____ of Chickamauga. _____ great battle _____ _____ _____ force, under _____ Rosecrans, the _____ _____ _____ _____ _____ _____ defeated and put to rout.

_____ _____ The Confederates _____ _____ and commit great outrages in _____ _____ _____ _____ _____ in Virginia. _____ _____ for _____ _____ _____ great battle impending.

_____ _____ Gen. Magruder _____ _____ the _____ _____ Gen. Weitzel and _____ _____

Sept. — Expedition of Capt. _____ to the Pamunky river, in _____ _____ _____ _____ _____ Yankee transport _____ _____ _____ _____ _____.

Sept. — Gen. Kirby S_____ _____ Little Rock, Ark. _____ _____ _____ _____ Little Rock occupied .... The Federals under Gen. ...... also occu.......

Sept. .... n with a force of 13,... ...... four ...... and twenty... transports, attacks the fort ...... bined..... Two of the gunboats are disabled and ca.... mounting eighteen guns, also two or three hundred prisoners. Another of the gunboats disabled and the entire expedition driven back and abandoned. The Confederate battery of six guns, manned by 42 men, with a support of 200 infantry. ... loss on the part of the Confederates. This is regarded the most brilliant exploit of the war.

Sept. 21. The Yankees make a raid on Bristol, Tenn, and burn the town.

Sept. 22. Cavalry fight near Madison Court House, Va. The enemy driven back.

Sept. 16. The Confederates 1200 strong, under Gen. Tom Green, attack a superior Federal force near the mouth of Red river, killing 200 and capturing 400 prisoners.

Sept. 26. Gen. Wheeler makes a cavalry raid in the rear of Rosencran's army, capturing many prisoners and destroying large amounts of Federal stores, wagon trains, &c.

Oct. 5. Both armies still confronting each other in and near Chattanooga. The Federals still entrenching and fortifying their position. The Confederates also entrenching and occupying Lookout Mountain commanding the river and railroad below and near Chattanooga. Rosencranz heavily reinforced by Burnsides, Hooker and Sherman. Artillery firing continues on both sides. Gen. Wheeler's cavalry continue to harass the enemy's rear. The reports of capture of enemy's supplies, unprecedented.

Oct. 9. Gen. Chalmers, with 1,200 men, attacks the enemy, 1,500 strong with six pieces of artillery, at ...... After a severe fight the enemy were driven ....

Oct. 10. Cavalry fight at ...... river, Va. Yankees defeated, with a loss of 100 prisoners left in our hands.

Oct. 15. A severe engagement took place at Bible ...., Tenn., also on the 11th at ...... Confederates defeated with a loss of 500 to 600 killed and wounded in both engagements.

Oct. 11. Gen. Stuart attacked the rear guard of the enemy at Brandy Station, driving them ...... a severe engagement. Confederate loss about ......

Oct. 12. Gen. Chalmers attacks the enemy at Collierville,

Miss. Confederates compelled to retire with a loss of about [...]. Few Yankee prisoners were captured by [...] and their trains saved.

Oct. 12. Engagement at Culpepper Court [...]. Five [...] prisoners captured.

Oct. 13.—Dismissal by President Davis of all the British consuls in the Confederate States, in consequence of [...] interference in behalf of British subjects, enrolled under the conscription laws.

Oct. 14—Confederate cavalry operations in the enemy's rear continue. Gen. Wheeler reports he crossed the river in the face of a division of the enemy at Cotton Port Ford, on the 30th, and proceeded in the direction of McMinnville, when after a sharp fight he captured a large train and 700 prisoners. The train was loaded with ammunition and other stores, and supposed to consist of 800 wagons, all which were burned. He then attacked Morganville, capturing 530 prisoners, and another large train, destroyed several bridges, an engine and a train of cars. He then moved to Shelbyville, where he captured a large amount of stores and burned them. Gen. Wheeler up to this date has destroyed an amount of wagons, stores, &c., which has no precedent in the annals of raiding.

Oct. 14.—Heavy skirmishing continues on the Rappahannock, Va., with varying success; the enemy generally retiring. Cavalry operations in Tennessee still continue. Gen. Williams meets with a severe revenge to the confederate arms near Jonesboro, Tenn.

Oct. [...] A large force of yankees, consisting of eleven regiments of cavalry with nine pieces of artillery advanced [...] and burned Wyatt, Miss. Confederate cavalry maintained several skirmishes with the enemy for many miles. The contest at times severe.

Oct. 15.—A severe cavalry fight took place between the Confederates and yankees, at Culleton Station, Va. Confederates lost about 500 killed and wounded. A confederate brigade thrown into confusion by a sudden attack of the yankees, and five pieces of artillery lost. The enemy withdrew.

SIEGE OF CHARLESTON.

...the following account of the situation from the ...
... Chronicle and Sentinel:

... was the gallant effort of the li'tle steamer ...
... the ... our waters. But ...
... I ... sincerely wish to report that the ...
... and that Lieut- ... and his companion is safe, having been rescued from the waters ...
... the enemy's ... and made prisoner of war.

The Yankees are busy, as ... and are perfect ... in ... work. They understand the manual of the pick and spade and the ... to perfection, and go through the motions as well as if they were executing the manual of arms in Hardee's school for the soldier.

Comparatively speaking, a calm has spread its broad ... or the waters of our bay. For sometime ... have the ... occasional booming and sullen roar of hostile guns ... has transpired to mar the serenity or ... the terrible calm which precedes the storm. Now and then, at stated intervals through the short ... days, the Yankee battery Gregory ... has thundered and hurled the bolts of death at Sumter or the sultry Fort Johnson or Battery ... But only now and then a puff of white smoke slowly curling away in fantastic wreaths and drifting idly over the bay ... that "gun answers ..."

Fort Sumter's ruined walls have received the greatest attention from the enemy's thunderer at Gregory's Hill. ... gun, heavy, battered and torn, she still ... crest ... "in the broad sunlight of a new ... deed ... her do 'Twas behind the ... of dilapidation and of no seeming protection when he dismantled ... ould be ... in the night time. 'Twas here that the thunders of the ... were first heard, and ... he ... booming ... tumbled ... here that Dupont and his never-to-be-forgotten ... armored iron turreted monitors ... his discomfiture ... and ... pierced, riddled and sent to "Davy Jones' locker." ... here that the glorious Charleston Battalion, the "brick boys," overturned Dahlgren's grand boating excursion ... his naval heroes to shame—illustrated the dear old city and won never fading laurels. Sumter! proud heroic ...! Sumter has withstood a terrible siege—has gone through an ordeal hitherto unknown to the history of war; and though the

_____ ___ fort has become a crumbling pile of shapeless ruins

> _____ _____ _____
> _____ __ ___ _____ _____,
> ___ _____ ___ __ __ _____ ___ ___,
> _____ ___ ____ _____ _____.

_____ _____ the _____ preserve ____ _____ _____,
___ ___ __ _____ __ the ____ __ ____ _____ _____ Jones
Island, Dixon's, Plumb, ____ ___ ___ ___ ____ _____,
___ _____ by the enemy. . On Dixon's arm, a narrow slip
running out, to the rear of Dixon's Island, a strong, formidable
_____ stockade has been built. On black Island, the Yankees
have erected two batteries, and Admiral Dahlgren has placed
obstructions in Light House Inlet to keep us from annoying
his Abolition craft. Here, when the jolly tars have nothing
else to do, two schooners armed with little speakers of the
Parrot order, amuse themselves by spitting fire and shell at
Secessionville. At times they become quite irate—and spend
some time as well as ammunition—doing nothing! In Stono
Bay there is also quite a fleet of transports, attended by a few
vessels of war. The Pawnee, determined to "have a finger in
the pie,"—"a place in the picture"—occasionally runs up the
Stono to within shelling distance of our western lines, hurls a
shell or two and then "skedaddles."

Batteries Gregg and Wagner have become more formidable
than ever. Every portion of these shattered and battle-scar-
red works has been remodelled and strengthened. Jagged,
torn and crumbling walls of sand have been re-fashioned by
the pliant hands of skilful engineers, and now loom up into
distinct and well defined outlines of strong, well built batteries, that bristle all over with guns of the heaviest calibre.
Many two hundred pounder Parrot guns have been mounted,
which command the channel or look significantly towards the
"doomed city." True, it is, they may deluge our beautiful
city with a constant shower of Greek fire; pour a rain of iron
hail upon her devoted head; transform the proud and lovely
to smouldering ashes and crumbling dust; may burn the "nest
of traitors;" consume the "hot bed of rebellion," but they
can never crush her spirit or pollute her ashes with their
vandal hoofs.

Let them burn Charleston then, if they will—appease the
raging fanatics of the North who shriek for her destruction. We can see her dear old walls totter and crumble and
___ _____ __ ___ behold our Queen City writhe in the

... the torture of ... the temples and ... we lisped our youthful prayers and sung our Sabbath hymns—gilded domes where art ... inscribed her ... and science reared a home—yes, we can ... see ... "home, sweet home," around whose ... hearth ... the ... of affection ...

A List of Killed, Wounded and Missing in the battles,
... es and Engagements of the War for the
... 1861, 1862, and 1863.

CONFEDERATE VICTORIES.

CONFEDERATE VICTORIES—Co...

Battles, Skirmishes and Engagements.	Date.	Confederates killed.	Confederates wounded.	Confederates captured.	Federals killed.	wounded.
Pensacola	November ...23	13	7		11	23
Near Vienna	November ...26					
An...la	December ...	8				3
Alleghany	December ... 13	20	96			
Woodsonville	December ...17	2	11		20	
Gen. Price's Retreat	Dec ...17-18-19	5	10	200	15	60
Chustenahlah	December ...26	18	32		250	178
Skirmish on Green River	December ...28	2	3		15	20
	1862.					
Port Royal River	January	7	10			
Middle Creek	January ...10	10	14			
Near Boston, Ky	January ...					
J... Island	January ...	5				
New Concord	February				5	
Near Galveston	February					
Near Savannah, Tenn. River	March	7	14			
Near New Madrid	March				18	
New Creek, Va	March	8				
Hampton Roads	March ...8-9	0	10		200	
Near Nashville	March					
Charleston	March					
St. Mary's River	March ...23				40	10
Warrenton, Va	March ...15	6	108		40	
Point Pleasant	March ...18					
Valverde	March ...21	86	148		230	500
Mosquito Inlet	March					
Winchester	March ...23	93	168	280	225	
Near Jefferson City	March ...27	3			78	130
Edisto Island	March ...29				11	
Rappahannock River	March ...29			3		
Jacksonville	March ...31	4	1			
Shiloh	April ...6-7	1728	8012	959		
Near Shiloh	April ...	4	6			
East Tennessee	April ...7					
Skirmishing Peninsula	April ...18	5	13	10	17	
Whitemarsh Island	April ...16					
Lee's Farm	April ...					
Fort Wright	April ...					
Pensacola	April ...	18				
Logan County	April ...	18	40			
Pittsburg Landing	April ...					
Cumberland Gap	April ...	27				
Barhamsville	May ...	7				10
Williamsburg	May ...	648	1109			
McDowell's	May ...	100	168		175	
Farmington	May ...					
Parkburg	May ...10-11					
Pollocksville	May ...					
Drury's Bluff	May ...					
City Point	May ...					
Near Corinth	May ...					
Near W...	May ...					
Searcy	May ...18-19			17		
St. Mark	May ...					
Front Royal	May ...					
Lewisburg	May ...	70	100			
Sunnett's Farm	May ...					
Winchester	May ...					
Hanover Court House	May ...26-27	39				

CONFEDERATE VICTORIES—Continued.

Battles, Skirmishes and Engagements.	Date.	Confederates Killed.	Confederates Wounded.	Confederates Captured.	Federals Killed.	Federals Wounded.	Federals Captured.
Galveston	January		20	50			160
Hartsville	January	15	70		10		
Fort McAllister	January				40		
Near Murfreesboro	January						
New Madrid	January	18					13
Charleston Harbor	January						
Fort Lowry	February		21				
Hartwood Church	February	25	4	13			
Fort							
Fort							
Spring Hill	March	4	58		10	187	
Near Jacksonville	March	16					
Fairfax Court House	March	10					
Fort	March	8			10		
Kelly's Ford	March	15	63		100		
Suffolk River	March	2					
Ponchatoula	March	25	11				
Brentwood	March	1	35		10	100	
Dranesville	April				60		
Brier Hill	April	5	1		5		
Charleston	April	4			5		
Pascagoula	April				10		
Big Bear Creek	April						
Kingston	April	14	12				
Straight's Cavalry Raid	April						
Near Tullahoma	May						
Battles of the Mississippi	May						
Plains store	May						
Near Fredericksburg	May						
Winchester	June						
Martinsburg	June		6				
Knoxville	June						
Mechanicsburg	June			18			
Strawberry Plains	June		7	13			
Near Pontotoc	June						
Berwick Bay	June		1	54			
Gettysburg	July	3000	1500		1000		
White Sulphur Springs	August	20	147				
Dry Creek	August		8	27			
Chickamauga	Sept. 20	1800	10	1880	3000		
Various skirmishes the last ten months		475	1580		880		

FEDERAL VICTORIES.

Battles, Skirmishes and Engagements	Date	Confederates Killed	Confederates Wounded	Confederates Captured	Federals Killed	Federals Wounded	Federals Captured
	1861						
Phillippi	June		4			2	
Booneville	June		20		24	63	
Carrick's Ford	July	44	57				
St. George	July	18	17			11	
Hatteras	August	12		691?			
Osceola	September 21		7		10	16	
Chapmansville	September	4	4				
Fredericktown	October						
Port Royal	November	11	48	3	3		
McCoy's Mill	November	7	8				
Capture of Col. Magoffin	December						
Drainsville	December 7	67	180		68	150	
Surrender of Fort Smith	April 26						
Surrender at Neosho	July	6					
Fredericktown			14	40		36	87
	1862						
Hanging Rock	January 5	5	5	5			
Fishing Creek	January	114	165	45	38	194	
Near Occoquan	January 2	20	9				
Blooms y	February	1			44	17	
Fort Henry	February	5	8	47	8		
Roanoke	February 7-8	36	87	62	35	214	
Cobb's Point	February 10	5	3		11		
Fort Donelson	February 14-16	231	1007	6079	446	1735	150
Winton	February	7					
Newbern	March	44	76	200	100	470	
Pea Ridge	March	100	300	200	500	1000	500
Cumberland Gap	March		1			2	
New Madrid	March	10	50			17	
South Mills	March	7			13	100	
Near Cumberland Gap	March		1			3	
Polk County	March	20				40	
	March 26	2			5	20	70
Fort Pulaski	April 11		4				
Island 10	April	3		5000	150	300	
Fort Jackson	April	34	115		500	500	
Fort Macon	April 25		14				
Gadsville	April 27-28	30	62				
Near Lebanon	May	20	66	45			
Lewisburg	May 23-24	46	104		53	179	
Garnett's Farm	May 31-June 2	25	12		59	74	
Naval Battle near Memphis	June	90	72				
Fayetteville	July	12					
Mt. Sterling	July	4	20		3	7	
Near Bolivar	July	3	11				
Orange Court House	August	7	101				
Fort Craig	September 14	65	230		13	30	
Near Opelousas	September 13-14	15	26	50	10		190
Iuka	September 19-20	200			168	542	
Corinth	October 3-4-5	1200	2500	2000	400	1830	300
Albemarle	October	19	15	500			
Williamston	November 2-4	4	30		7	39	
In various skirmishes during the last ten months		990	2560	2000	500	1290	500
Abbeville, Miss.	December 1	5	5		10		
Water Valley	December 3				6	14	
Whitehill	December 16-17	236	466		500	900	
Davis Mills	December 21	12	62		20	60	

Battles, Skirmishes and Expeditions.	Date.	Confederates Killed.	Confederates Wounded.	Confederates Captured.	Federals Killed.	Federals Wounded.	Federals Captured.
Whitney's Mill's	December ..			112			
Parker's Cross Roads	December .. 31	60	150	300	65		
	1863.						
Springfield	January	20	90				
Arkansas Post	January ..8	60	490	3700			
Fort Donelson	February ..4	27	81	300	16		
Richmond, La.	February						
Tuscumbia	March			80			
Bradyville	March	3	17				12
Milton	March 4..14	20	190				
Franklin	April ....9..10	23	75		11		
Camp Bisland	April ....13..14						
Tuscumbia	April	15					
Fayetteville	April	6	15				
Suffolk	April 19				14		
Grierson's Raid	April						
Cape Girardeau	April 26	5	20	65			
Hamilton's Crossing	April	200	470	193	600	150	
Bayou Pierre	May	85	370	380	100	490	
Raymond	May	47	180		300	200	
Jackson	May	250	579		4	150	
Baker's Creek	May	477	190			150	
Big Black Bridge	May						
Upperville	June						
Hoover's Gap	June	50	300	203			
Hanover Court House	June	10	20		5		
Vicksburg	July		3750	7800	1330	4200	
Helena	July	150	435	1130	90	374	
Port Hudson	July	500	517	6300	2000	3000	
Jackson	July	117				600	
Morris Island	September..	100				420	
Chattanooga	September..						
Various skirmishes during the last ten months							

COMPARATIVE STATEMENT

OF THE

KILLED, WOUNDED AND PRISONERS

on both sides, from the commencement of the war to September 1st, 1864, including the fight at Chickamauga, Sept. 19-20, 1863:

	Confed. killed.	Confed. wound.	Confed. prisoners.	Total.
1861.	1,279	3,935	2,773	7,987
1862.	14,566	47,904	16,076	77,546
1863.	12,004	48,200	71,411	131,832
	28,147	88,439	89,849	217,463

Confederates died from disease and sickness from commencement of war to present time, — 150,000

	Fed. killed.	Fed. wounded.	Fed. prisoners.	Total.
1861.	4,123	9,701	6,794	38,709
1862.	30,575	61,970	45,800	138,345
1863.	15,312	53,981	31,864	102,625
	49,966	132,745	89,009	283,720

Federals died from disease and sickness from commencement of war to present time. 200,000

NAPOLEON AND THE MASSACRE OF DECEMBER.—Mr. Kings-lake, in his Invasion of the Crimea, reviews the history of Napoleon III, with a caustic pen. Of the massacre of the Boulevards on the 4th of December, 1852, speaking of the slaughter from the Rue de Sentier to the western extremity of the Boulevard Montmartre, he observes that the slayers were thousands of soldiers, and the slain were a number that will never be counted ; but among all of these slayers and slain there was no one combatant.

There was no fight, no riot, no fray, no quarrel, no dispute. What happened was a slaughter of unarmed men, women and children. Where they lay the dead bore witness. Corpses lying apart struck deeper into people's memory than the dead who were lying in heaps. Some were haunted with the look of an old man with silver hair, whose only weapon was the umbrella which lay at his side. Some shuddered because of seeing the gay idler of the Boulevard sitting dead against the wall of a house, and scarce parted from the cigar which lay on the ground near his hand. Some carried in their minds the sight of a printer's boy, leaning back against a shop front, because, though the boy was killed, the proof-sheets which he was carrying had remained in his hands, and were red with his blood, and were fluttering in the wind.

One grand object was gained by these military operations. They effectually stopped the laugh against the silent, torpid man who had undertaken to succeed his uncle. The comic side of the plot of December 2d, passed quite out of view. The new power was from that moment a thing which all men respect "a great fact." One of the colonels engaged, declared that his regiment alone killed 2,400 men. Paris on the 5th Decem-looked like a city struck down by a plague. The Parisians are not afraid to look on street fighting, but an English writer says that some of the people retreating from the scenes of slaughter were a livid hue which he had never before seen.

Thus, then, Louis Bonaparte was delivered, once and forever, from the ridicule which until that day had incessantly pursued him. France was effectually cowed, and now was the time to disarm her. In a few weeks twenty-six thousand five hundred men, selected in the belief that they were citizens who would dare something for the honor and liberty of their country, were siezed and transported without form of law under a retro-operative decree of the plotters.

These were the acts by which Louis Napoleon founded his power, and thus he was enabled to sit, like the Czar, and gov-

the movements of the police, the regiments, the cannon, and the ships of France, by his personal will.

———————◇———————

WELLS IN THE DESERTS.—The French are acquiring great influence among the desert tribes of Algeria, by the introduction of useful European arts, especially that of boring for water. Beneath certain sections of the Great Desert, there is either a subterranean lake or river; and this has been long known to the native Arabs, among whom there are professional well-sinkers, who form a numerous body, enjoying much consideration, their work being of a very dangerous character. They excavate in the ground, and when they reach a certain depth they know by the color of the soil if water is below. A thin crust covers the subterranean stream, and when it is broken the water in it rushes up with the velocity of petroleum in American oil-wells. In the south of Algeria, the well-sinkers endeavor to find a subterranean stream, which is sometimes tapped at the depth of about 550 feet. Colonel Dumas, of the French army, thus describes the mode of excavating them :—

"The section is in a square form. One workman alone works at it; and, as he advances, he supports the sides with four planks of palmtree. But certain infallible signs—for instance, when the soil becomes black and moist—he knows that he is near the spring. He then fills his ears and nostrils with wax, that he may not be suffocated by the uprising deluge of water, and fastens a rope under his arms, having previously arranged to be drawn up on a given signal. At the last stroke of the pick, the water often rises so rapidly that the unhappy well-sinker is drawn up insensible. These inexhaustible springs are the common property of the village which has discovered them and are conveyed to the gardens in conduits of hollowed palm-tree trunks. It is these springs which are the foundation of the greater number of "oases of Sahara." In 1853, when French conquest had extended to the vast and mysterious solitude called the Great Desert, well-boring and sinking apparatus were introduced, and astonished the Arabs by their simplicity and effectiveness. In the five years ending 1859—'60, fifty wells have been opened; 30,000 palms and 1000 fruit trees have been planted; many oases have revived

from the ruin caused by a failure of springs ; and two villages
have been created in the Desert ; the total expense not having
been much more than £20,000 sterling which has been repaid
by taxes and voluntary contributions from the Arabs.   Col
Dumas observes :   " Such works give us ten times more influence than our military victories.   The waters bubbling up
from these borings are generally charged with sulphate of
soda, magnesia, and lime, either as a chloride or a sulphate,
which makes them bitter and salt ; but the Arabs are only
too glad to have any kind of water, and the palms and other
vegetable products of the Desert thrive on it."   The borings
of Sidi-Sliman and K'Sour present the curious phenomenon
of live fish. A parallel to this case was reported by M. Ayme,
governor of the oasen of Egypt, to a scientific society in
France.   In clearing a well 325 feet deep, he said " he had
found fish fit for cooking."   The French propose to extend
these wells into the Desert, so as to unite the rich oases of
Touat—ou the route to Timbuctoo—with Algéria, and then
direct the stream of overland commerce into its ancient channel by Algeria.

REMARKABLE EVENTS IN THE WORLD'S HISTORY DURING THE YEAR 1863.

January 5. Immense gold fields discovered in New Zealand,

January 9. Frightful accident at Locarno, Italy, by the falling of the roof of a church ; 53 lives lost.

January 20. Great distress among the cotton operatives of England on account of the American Revolution.

January 21, 22. Battle between the French and Mexicans at Tampico, Mexico. The French evacuate the city.

Jan. 30. A Revolution breaks out in Poland against the Russian government. Gen'l Langiewicz leads the Poles, and is appointed Dictator.

February 16. Accident on the Southern Railroad, Miss ; 7 persons killed and wounded.

February 19. Accident at Chunkey river, on Southern Railroad ; over 50 lives lost.

February 23, 24. Battle of Coatepeque, San Salvador, South America, between the troops of Guatemala and San Salvador. The Guatemalian army defeated, with a loss of 500 killed and wounded ; loss of San Salvadors only 60 killed and wounded.

February 20. Massacre of whites by the Indians in Gillespie county, Texas, 7 persons killed. An underground railroad of four miles completed, by tunneling under the streets in London, England.

February 24, 25. A terrible tornado passed over Barry's Landing, Opelousas, La. ; 5 lives lost, a large amount of property destroyed.

February 28. Mrs. Ann Singleton died at Williamsburg, South Carolina, aged 130 years.

February 20. Battle between French and Mexicans at El Organo, Mexico ; the French defeated.

March 1. Indian massacre in northern Texas ; several whites killed.

March 2. Political riot at Calamut, Mich. ; several persons killed and wounded.

March 8. Accident on Southern Railroad, Miss. ; 3 lives lost.

March 8. A terrible tornado passed over Middle Tennessee; several lives lost, and large amount of property destroyed.

March 19. Destructive fire in Richmond, Va.; a large amount of government property destroyed.

March — Riot in Detroit, Mich., between whites and blacks; several persons killed and wounded.

March 13. Fatal explosion in a confederate laboratory at Richmond, Va.; 35 females killed and 31 wounded.

March 10. Marriage of the Prince of Wales with the Princess Alexandria of Denmark, in London, England: The ceremonies were attended with great pomp and magnificence; three ladies killed and many wounded in the great rush attending the festivities.

March 14. Riot between whites and blacks at Oil Springs, Canada West.

March 15. D. B. H. Starr hung by a vigilance committee in Montgomery, Ala.

March 17. The French army attacks the city of Puebla, Mexico.

March 16. Battle between the Poles and Russians at Leulek, Poland; the latter were defeated, with a loss of 450.

March 19. The steamer Georgiana, with a valuable cargo, wrecked while attempting to run the blockade at Charleston, North Carolina.

March 22. Massacre of whites by Indians, on the overland route, Utah Territory.

March 26, 27. The siege of Puebla, Mexico, continues; the French repulsed, with a loss of 800 killed and wounded.

March 28. Tragedy at Beverly, Mass.; a man poisons his wife, father and mother. The great engineering enterprise of tunnelling the Alps in Switzerland, for railroad purposes, has been in progress for five years; only one mile has been bored in that time; it is calculated that the remaining distance of eleven miles will be completed in ten years.

March 31. Official information has been received of Col. Connor's severe battle and splendid victory on Bear river, Washington territory, U. S. After a forced march of one hundred and forty miles, in mid winter and through deep snows, in which seventy-six of his men were disabled by frozen feet, he and his gallant band of only two hundred attacked a party of three hundred Indian warriors in their stronghold, and after a hard-fought battle of four hours, destroyed the entire band, leaving two hundred and twenty four dead upon the field. Our loss was fourteen killed and forty-nine wounded.

These Indians had murdered several and during the winter, and were a part of the same band who have been massacreing emigrants on the overland routes for the last fifteen years, and the principal actors and leaders in the horrid crimes of the past summer.

April 4. Soldiers mutiny in Portland, several killed.

April 7. Great Democratic meeting, New York city against the Lincoln administration in favor of peace.

April 13. Riot in New York city between whites and negroes.

April 13. The Polish Revolution continues to increase. Battle between Poles and Russians at Suwalki, Poland, 200 Russians killed.

April 16. Riot at Halifax, Nova Scotia, between citizens and soldiers, several persons killed.

April — The British man-of-war Orpheus wrecked on the coast of New Zealand, 130 lives lost.

April 18. Bloody riot at Danville, Illinois, several killed.

April 18. Massacre of whites by Indians in northern Minnesota.

April 22. Newspaper office in Sacramento city destroyed by a mob of soldiers.

April 21. R. E. Dixon shot dead in Richmond, Va., by R. O. Ford. Gold selling at 600 per cent. in the confederate States.

April 23. Accident on the Richmond and Danville Railroad, Virginia; 12 persons killed and wounded.

April 27. Steamer Ada Hancock exploded her boiler near San Pedro, California. 40 persons killed and wounded.

May — Terrible earthquake at Modena, Italy; over 800 persons perished; the city destroyed.

May 2. Accident on Wilmington and Weldon Railroad, North Carolina, 5 persons killed and wounded.

May 5. C. L. Vallandigham arrested by order of Gen'l Burnside, at his residence in Dayton, Ohio; a riot occurs, in which the people tried to prevent his arrest.

May 6. Steamer Majestic burned on the Mississippi river, 60 lives lost.

May 16. The French under Gen'l Forey, capture the city of Puebla, Mexico, after a protracted siege. The French army advances on the city of Mexico.

May 26, 28. Great storm in the Gulf of Mexico; immense loss of property on the coast; the steamship Soler wrecked.

June 3. Terrible earthquake at Manilla, Phillipine Islands, 2,000 persons perished.

June — Indian hostilities commence in Minnesota.

June 10. The French under Gen'l Forey occupy the city of Mexico.

July 1. Slavery abolished in the State of Missouri by the Legislature, after the year 1870.

July 8. Thomas Patrick Kendrick, Archbishop of Baltimore, died in Baltimore. Gold at a premium of 12 for 1 in the confederacy.

July 13, 14, 15. Terrible riots in New York city. The people resist Lincoln's draft; over 218 persons killed and wounded, mostly negroes; a large amount of property destroyed. Riots also occurred in Boston, Jersey city and other Northern cities. The Polish Revolution is gaining ground; four battles took place during the month, in which the Poles were successful.

July 27. Great fire in Havana; loss $11,000,000.

July 25. Gen'l Sam Houston died in Huntsville, Texas.

July 26. Gen. Crittenden died at Frankfort, Ky., aged 77 years.

July 28. Hon. Wm. L. Yancey died at Montgomery, Ala., aged 49 years.

August 1. Riot in Keokuk, Iowa, between Democrats and Union men; several persons killed.

August 4. The slaughter of a Confederate family near Island 10, Tenn., by a yankee and a party of negroes.

August 5. Steamer Ruth burned on the Mississippi river. 30 lives lost.

www.ingramcontent.com/pod-product-compliance
Lightning Source LLC
Chambersburg PA
CBHW032018010726
47493CB00007B/2461